DATE DUE			

30645

920
ASH

Ashabranner, Brent
K.

People who make a
difference.

People Who Make a Difference

People Who
Make a Difference

Brent Ashabranner

Photographs by Paul Conklin

Cobblehill Books

Dutton • New York

Library of Congress Cataloging-in-Publication Data
Ashabranner, Brent K., date.
People who make a difference / Brent Ashabranner : photographs by
Paul Conklin.
p.   cm.
Bibliography: p.
Includes index.
Summary: Describes the life and work of several men and women of various
ages, circumstances, and occupations who, by their caring and concern, are
helping to make a difference to those in need, the environment, and on a
personal level.
ISBN 0-525-65009-1
1. United States—Biography—Juvenile literature.   2. Biography—20th
century—Juvenile literature.   [1. United States—Biography.
2. Biography.]   I. Conklin, Paul, ill.   II. Title.
CT217.A63   1989   920.073—dc20
[B]   [920]   89-34593   CIP   AC

Published in the United States by
E. P. Dutton, New York, N.Y.,
a division of Penguin Books USA Inc.
Published simultaneously in Canada by
Fitzhenry & Whiteside Limited, Toronto
Designer: Joy Taylor
Printed in the United States of America
First edition
10   9   8   7   6   5   4   3   2   1

For Giancarlo
who makes a difference

Contents

People Who Make a Difference

Ron Cowart of Dallas.

Everyday Heroes

THIS IS a book about heroes. I say that knowing full well that the men and women I have written about would be astonished to hear themselves described as heroes. Who are they? A Vietnam veteran, now a policeman, who spends all of his time on duty and off helping to improve the lives of Southeast Asian refugees in Dallas. A woman who helps paroled women offenders find a secure place in society. A Capuchin friar in a small Eastern city who has organized one of the nation's most successful programs for housing the homeless and assisting them in finding jobs. An eighty-three-year-old woman who devotes her life to saving endangered species of sea turtles. These people and the others in this book have found some way to make the world around them a better place.

In *The Hero in America* Dixon Wecter defined heroes as people with an unwavering sense of duty and determination to "translate the dream into act." He was writing about Washington, Franklin, Jefferson, Jackson, Lincoln, Wilson, and Franklin Roosevelt. "None of these epic leaders left the Republic as he found it," says Wecter.

Years later, Robert Kennedy, in his writings and speeches, made the same points about heroism, although he did not use the word hero, and he was not talking about America's epic leaders. He was talking about ordinary people in ordinary walks of life.

"Few will have the greatness to bend history," Kennedy wrote in *To Seek a Newer World,* "but each of us can work to change a small portion of events, and in the total of all those acts will be written the history of this generation. . . . It is from numberless diverse acts of courage and belief that human history is shaped."

In our years of writing and photographing books about America, Paul Conklin and I have met many men and women who are the kind of people Robert Kennedy was talking about, the people who make a difference. You will meet some of them in the pages ahead.

1

Helping Those
Most in Need of Help

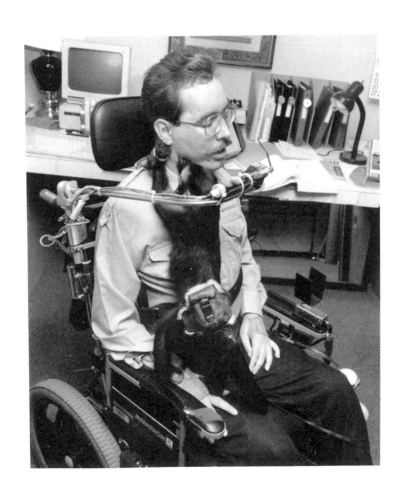

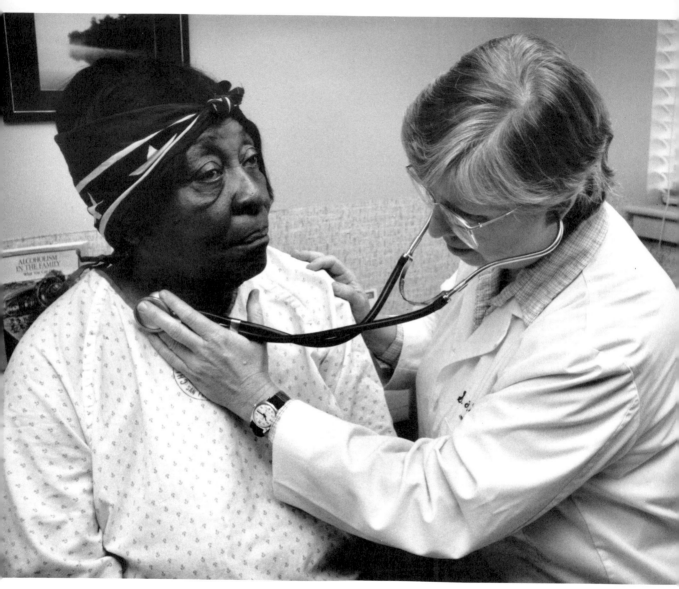

Dr. Anne Brooks with a patient.

"I Receive Love"

TUTWILER is a little town in Mississippi, about twelve hundred people, mostly black, mostly poor. It is located in Tallahatchie County, that part of the Mississippi River Delta where cotton has always been the economic staple of life and still is. Now, however, many of the plantations are fighting bankruptcy, and many of the farms have been foreclosed by the bank or are teetering on the brink of foreclosure. The per capita income of Tutwiler is about five thousand dollars a year, less than one-half the national average.

The residential areas of Tutwiler are pleasant enough, but when you are driving the back roads around the town, your first reaction is, can this be the United States? The shacks that dot the flat delta country are unpainted, falling apart, with privies in the rear, and rusted-out cars and other junk in the yards. Inside, the shacks are even worse; the walls of some of them have been turned black by years of wood smoke seeping from leaky stoves.

The health and medical needs of Tutwiler and its immediate area are almost without limit. Malnutrition is at the heart of the problem because in most houses there is not enough food, not the right kind of food, and no knowledge of what the right diet is. Diabetes, high blood pressure, infection: you name the disease; Tutwiler probably has it. Farm accidents, car accidents result in damaged bodies. Two statistics are especially dismaying: infant mortality is twice the national average; so is teenage pregnancy.

Tutwiler had a doctor once, but he left for greener pastures over ten years ago. After that, people doctored themselves or journeyed to one of the few doctors in other parts of the county if they could. The Tutwiler town council advertised for a doctor to replace the one who left, but no one answered the ads. What did a place like Tutwiler have to offer?

And then one day the mayor of the little town received a letter from a doctor. The letter did not come in response to an advertisement because the town council had long ago given up hope in ads. The letter was from Dr. Anne Brooks, and it just seemed to come from out of the blue. But there was a question in the letter that excited the mayor, the town council, and everyone else who heard about it. The question was this: would the people of Tutwiler be interested in Dr. Brooks coming to their town and opening a medical clinic?

Were they interested? They were *very, very* interested as the mayor's immediate response made quite clear. In her initial letter Dr. Brooks had not mentioned that she was also a Roman Catholic nun in the order of Sisters of the Holy Names of Jesus and Mary. Would that make a difference to the mayor and town council? It would not make a difference, they assured her. Tutwiler was Baptist country, no doubt about that, and Sister Anne Brooks might be the only Catholic in town. But Dr. Anne Brooks would also be the only physician in town.

Dr. Brooks came to Tutwiler in August, 1983, and set up her practice in the health clinic that had remained vacant since the departure of the last doctor. One of her first acts was to create a single waiting room so there would be no separation of black and white patients as there had been when the clinic was last in operation. That single act sent a clear message to the people of Tutwiler: everyone was welcome, and there

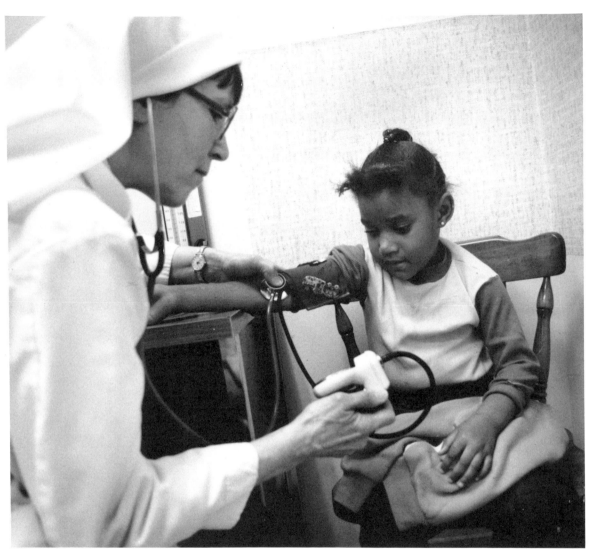

Sister Zenon D'Astous works with a young patient.

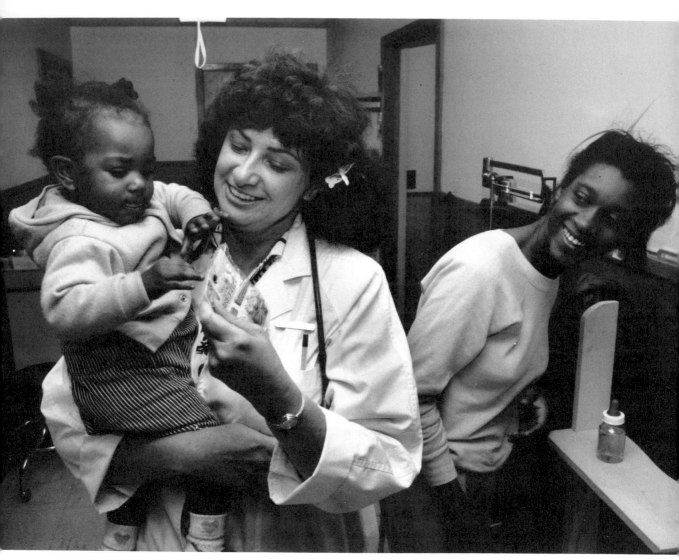

Ruth Vitko, a former clinic volunteer, tries to get a smile out of a baby.

would be no double standard in the dispensing of health care at the new clinic.

As quickly as possible Dr. Brooks put together a three-part staff—medical, office and clerical, and social outreach—to support the work of the clinic. She recruited several well-qualified Catholic sisters—including registered nurses and a laboratory technician—and hired twelve local lay workers.

"We can have a staff like this because they work for just a fraction of what professionals with their qualifications can make in hospitals and private clinics," says Dr. Brooks, referring to her sister colleagues. Dr. Brooks herself receives only a subsistance income of a few hundred dollars a month.

The newly reopened clinic was soon functioning at capacity with as many as fifty patients coming on some days, the monthly total running as high as seven hundred. The clinic is open for visits both morning and afternoon, but even at night people come to the big two-story house where Dr. Brooks and the other nuns live. In addition, Dr. Brooks spends a part of every day making house visits and answering emergency calls that may come at any time of the day or night.

"There are many problems," Dr. Brooks says and repeats for emphasis, "but the main one is malnutrition and its side effects—diabetes, anemia, high blood pressure, depression."

A major reason for malnutrition is the pervasive poverty of the area, and, as Dr. Brooks points out, a food stamp program that averages seventy-eight cents per meal does little to help the situation. The clinic has set up nutrition counseling and classes, and part of the outreach program has been to get people to return to school to continue their education.

Poverty presents Dr. Brooks with another problem. "These are proud people," she says, referring to her patients. "If they can't pay for our services—and many just don't have the cash—they won't come to the clinic. Their pride, their dignity won't let them. But I want them to come when they need us."

Dr. Brooks's answer to this problem is to let her patients pay the fifteen-dollar-clinic-visit fee and laboratory fees when they can and in many cases to take payment in kind. Such payment takes the form of doing chores at the clinic and sometimes of whatever the person can offer.

"We have been paid in peaches, collard greens, homemade cakes, and even catfish," says Dr. Brooks.

Fortunately, Medicare pays a portion of the costs incurred by many of the patients. But the clinic still runs at a deficit every year because, finally, many people simply cannot make payment or full payment. Dr. Brooks and other staff members have had to cover the deficit by soliciting donations from friends around the country. So far they have been successful.

THE LETTER that started it all—the letter from Dr. Brooks to the Tutwiler town council—was by no means from out of the blue. It was, in fact, but the last link in a long and remarkable chain that stretched from Anne Brooks's girlhood in a Catholic boarding school in Florida to a poverty-stricken little Mississippi town desperate for medical help.

She was born in 1938 in Washington, D.C., the only child of a Navy captain father and a mother who became a severe alcoholic. By the time she was ten, the family had collapsed, and, although neither she nor her parents were Catholic, her father placed her in a Catholic boarding school in Key West, Florida.

"The nuns at the school provided the love, meaning, and stability that I desperately needed in my life at that time," Anne Brooks says.

By the time she was eleven, she had made up her mind that she wanted to be a nun, and she never wavered from that early resolve. She became a nun in 1955 at the age of seventeen. That same year she was stricken with rheumatoid arthritis, a painful and crippling disease of the joints and adjacent muscles. By the time she took her final vows in the Sisters of the Holy Names of Jesus and Mary at age twenty-four, she was in almost constant pain and confined to a wheelchair most of the time.

Nevertheless, the young nun earned a degree in elementary education and for most of the next sixteen years worked as a teacher and principal in Catholic schools in Florida. Over the years, however, there

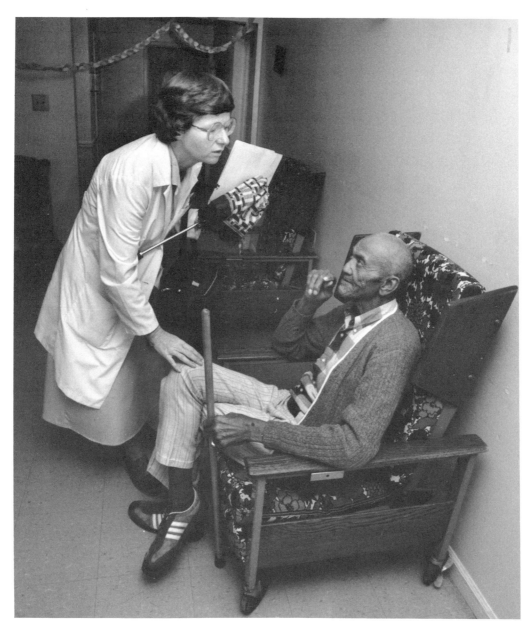

Sister Cora Lee Middleton visits an elderly shut-in in Tutwiler, Mississippi.

Dr. Brooks drops in on a patient she has helped often.

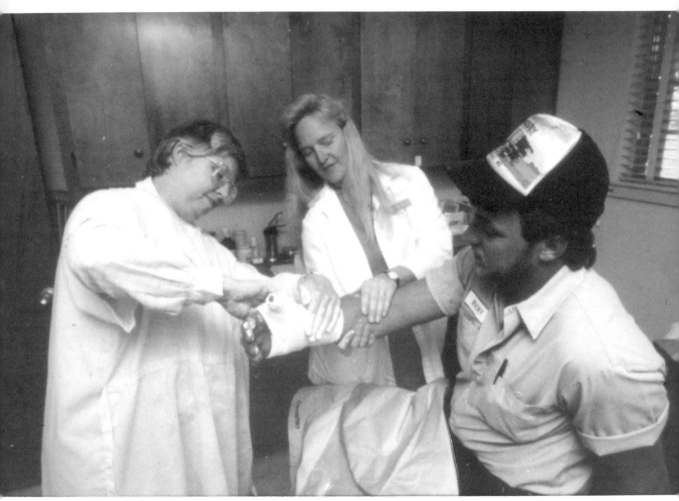

Dr. Brooks and assistant put on a cast.

grew in her a desire to do more, to work with people of greater need, particularly in the area of health care. She began by doing volunteer work at a health clinic in Clearwater, Florida, and was moved by the amount of good work going on and the seriousness of the needs of the poor who came to the clinic. Soon thereafter she petitioned the supervisor of her order for permission to work full time in the health field, and her request was approved.

In 1972 Anne Brooks met Dr. John Upledger, an osteopath and founder of the St. Petersburg Free Clinic. When Dr. Upledger told her that he could free her from the wheelchair and make her free of pain, she could only laugh in disbelief. But Dr. Upledger became her doctor and teacher, treating her with procedures of osteopathic medicine, including nutrition and exercise programs. Within six months she no longer needed her wheelchair; today, the pain sometimes disappears, sometimes comes back, but her walk is normal and healthy.

Osteopathy is a system of therapy based, in part, on manipulation of the body's bones and muscles. For many years osteopathy was not considered to be a part of the profession of medicine. Today, however, osteopaths or D.O.'s receive medical training that is similar to that received by M.D.'s.

In 1978, at the age of forty, Anne Brooks decided to become a doctor, a D.O. or Doctor of Osteopathy. Her commitment to a life of service in health care was now a total one, and Dr. Upledger urged her to enroll as a medical student at Michigan State University, where he had become a member of the staff. Once more, she obtained the permission of her order for a career change and became a student of osteopathy at Michigan State. In 1983, she graduated as Dr. Anne Brooks.

To finance her medical study at Michigan State University she applied for and received a scholarship from the National Health Service Corps. A condition of the scholarship is that the recipient practice medicine for four years in a medically deprived area of the United States. After her graduation, Dr. Brooks had an opportunity to survey such areas in the southern United States. One of her visits was to the Mississippi Delta, and one of the towns she looked at was Tutwiler. So when her letter came to

17

the Tutwiler town council, it was not a stab in the dark. She was looking for a place where she was really needed, and she knew that Tutwiler was such a place.

In 1987 Dr. Brooks completed her four years of service as required by her scholarship from the National Health Service Corps. She is now free to leave Tutwiler at any time she chooses, but she has no intention of leaving. "I have patients from fifteen different counties," she told me. "The word has gone out that I can 'fix backs.'" This is a humorous reference to her skills as an osteopath in a land where chopping cotton and planting vegetable crops are the main ways of making a living. "There is so much to be done here."

"You have said that you receive much more than you give in Tutwiler," I reminded Dr. Brooks. "What is it you receive?"

"I receive love," she answered simply.

"You give love, too," I said.

"Yes," she said, "and I receive it back a hundredfold. Those are good terms."

A Very Special
Fighting Machine

THE Ed Parker Karate Studio in Pasadena, California, has a tranquil Oriental look on the outside. Inside, it is cramped and the few pieces of furniture well worn and a bit shabby, but on the walls are photographs of famous Hollywood personalities who have worked out or trained at the studio, including Bruce Lee. On our first visit, the studio was full of noise with the arrival of young people for a workout session.

We had come for that session, but first we went to the office of Frank Trejo, manager of the studio. Frank is a big man, too big for his small, cluttered office. The office walls were filled with diplomas showing his progress in karate. He is sixth level Black Belt, which puts him near the top of the karate discipline. Trophies he had won in national and international competition were scattered around the office, including some on the floor.

"I'm a mean, mean fighting machine," he said, with a smile.

We were at the studio because two weeks earlier I had seen Frank on the NBC "Today Show" drilling a group of severely handicapped students in karate exercise. It had been an impressive sight, and I wanted to see it for myself. Now, in the short time before the workout, I wanted to dig into Frank's background and learn how he came to be a professional in karate. Frank is outgoing, talks easily and fast. All I had to do was ask a couple of questions and then keep quiet and listen.

Frank comes from a Mexican-American family. He grew up in Pasadena, but his mother and father were migrant farm workers. "We were poor, my whole family," he said. "I'm still poor. My grandfather and uncle were boxers during the Depression. Me and my brother didn't have much choice but to fight, too. I was a real skinny, lanky kid, but by fourteen I was a pretty good little fighter. Karate always fascinated me. There was something mystical about it. The first time I came into this place, I knew this was going to be my life."

I asked about the Ed Parker studio. Ed Parker, I was told, was one of the legendary figures in karate; there are Ed Parker studios all over the country.

"When I was sixteen," Frank continued, "I got a job at a car wash so that I could give my brother karate lessons. Then I would learn all the moves from him. I would say, 'How does that go?' And we'd go over and over all the moves. In '69 I answered an Ed Parker newspaper ad for instructors. I got the job! They taught me, and I taught beginners. 'This is the block. This is the punch. This is the kick.' Man, I taught that stuff ten hours a day. But along the way I became a teacher, a real teacher."

Just then one of Frank's helpers came to the door to say that the class was ready, and we went into the workout room. About twenty boys and girls were there, dressed in white karate workout uniforms. All this group was from Lincoln School in the nearby town of San Gabriel. I knew from talking earlier to Jan Taylor, a psychologist at the school, that all were students in the special education program, severely handicapped in some way. Some had Down's syndrome with differing degrees of mental retardation; others had cerebral palsy with speech, hearing, and muscular control problems and in some cases mental retardation; still others were autistic, with special learning and movement problems. This was one of eight special groups from different schools that worked out with Frank during the week—130 students in all.

20

Frank Trejo with students and teachers.

Frank Trejo with a group of his Creative Physical Fitness students.

I also knew that many physical therapists, physical education specialists, and medical experts were skeptical and pessimistic that young persons with such severe handicaps could learn activities that called for the exercise of memory and group coordination.

And then I watched Frank Trejo in action. With the help of two assistants, he got the group of students into rows. They began with the traditional bow of respect to the instructor. After that Frank took them through a series of karate warm-up exercises: neck rotations, hip and waist rotations and bending, leg stretches and squats, and other loosening-up maneuvers. After that they practiced the "horse," a stability stance in which the legs are set about twice as far apart as shoulder width. They practiced blocks, punches, and hand movements, all designed to develop upper body dexterity.

Frank, in his black workout uniform, his voice loud as he called out instructions, was like a magnet for the students' attention. They followed his every move and did their best to imitate. What was most obvious of all was that they were thoroughly enjoying what they were doing and enjoying being a part of this activity together. Frank was patient but insistent that they do the exercises correctly. The assistants worked with individuals, and from time to time Frank would give one of the students his individual attention.

Jan Taylor was there from Lincoln School, as were some teachers from other schools that had groups training with Frank. I talked with them and found they were all convinced that the karate program was helping the young participants in many ways: improved motor skills, longer attention span, improved ability to follow instructions, more stamina and strength.

"And a better feeling about themselves, an improved self-image," Jan said. "That may be most important of all."

Later, when the students had returned to school and the studio was quiet, I settled down with Frank again. "How did this start?" I asked him. "What made you think you could teach karate to boys and girls like the ones who were just here?"

The idea didn't start with him, Frank said, but rather with Lauren

Frank Trejo gives special attention to one of his students.

Tewes, the actress who for years was one of the stars of the "Love Boat" television series in the role of the cruise director. "She was one of my karate students," he said, "and she also worked with handicapped children in the Very Special Arts Festival that is held in Los Angeles every year. It's kind of like the Special Olympics for handicapped kids, but it focuses on singing, painting, dancing, things like that.

"Lauren got the idea that maybe I could train a group of handicapped kids to perform karate in the Very Special Arts Festival. I had my doubts. I was really skeptical. And then I started hearing people saying it couldn't be done. Well, I had a learning disorder when I was in school. I didn't know how to read. Oh, I could read the words, but I couldn't put them together to make sense. I finally taught myself how to read six years ago.

"And in 1983, I got a broken neck from a blow to the head in a karate tournament. I was paralyzed on my right side. Surgery fixed that, but I had to build myself back up through karate exercises.

"So I figured I knew something about the problems these kids have. And I didn't like people saying no one could teach them karate skills. I figured, I'm a teacher. I can try. But then the first tryout was arranged, on the baseball field at Pasadena High School, and I stood out there in front of those kids, and I said to myself, what have I got myself into now? But by the end of that first session I could see that they could learn and wanted to learn and liked it, and I started working with them twice a week. We worked for about five months, and then we put on a program in the Very Special Arts Festival. I'm told it was a big success."

It was, in fact, a huge success and led to the program that is now going on in the eight schools. Frank has worked hard to find and develop those special features of karate that are most appropriate for severely handicapped young people. The program has been given the name Creative Physical Fitness, and it is attracting nationwide attention.

I knew that Frank had given all of his time to the program on a volunteer basis. "You may become rich and famous," I said.

"I'm still poor," he said again.

Helping Hands

YOU ARE thirsty. A cold drink is in the refrigerator ten feet away, but it might as well be ten miles away. You can't move a muscle to reach it. Your nose itches until your eyes water, but you can't lift a hand to scratch. You want to watch a videotape, but all you can do is look helplessly at your VCR across the room and wait until someone comes to put in the cassette.

Your name is Mitch Coffman, and you are a prisoner in your own body. Your mind is clear and sharp; you can talk and move your head, but you can't move any other part of your body. Like almost a hundred thousand other men and women in the United States, you are a quadriplegic, totally paralyzed from the neck down.

Mitch Coffman's entry into the world of the quadriplegic came on a day that should have been a happy one. He was returning from a party to celebrate his thirtieth birthday when his car skidded on a bridge and went into a spin. Mitch was thrown out with an impact that broke his neck.

When Mitch regained consciousness, he came instantly face-to-face with a terrible reality: he had suffered permanent damage to his spine between the third and fifth cervical vertebrae. He would be paralyzed for the rest of his life.

After months of physical therapy, Mitch regained enough movement in his left hand to operate the control for an electric wheelchair. And he was more fortunate than most quadriplegics because he was able to move into a government-subsidized apartment building especially equipped for people with severe physical disabilities. The building has ramps instead of stairs, roll-in showers, light switches and other electrical and kitchen equipment that are easy to reach and operate. Attendants are also on duty at all times. Still, there were endless hours every day and night when Mitch was alone in his apartment waiting, waiting for the simplest tasks to be performed for him.

And then one day a stranger arrived in Mitch's little apartment. She was only eighteen inches tall, weighed but a furry six pounds, and communicated in excited squeaks and endless trills. But she could open the refrigerator door and bring Mitch a cold drink or a sandwich. She could scratch his nose with a soft cloth when it itched. She could put a videotape in the VCR. She could do dozens of other things for him that he could not do for himself.

The stranger was a black and brown capuchin monkey, and her improbable name was Peepers. Almost as important as what she could do for him was the fact that she was there, a companion, a constant presence in the apartment where, for most of the long hours of long days, there had been only Mitch.

"It took us months to learn to live together," Mitch explains as Peepers sits quietly in his lap. "Now I can't imagine living without her."

THE MODEST quarters of Helping Hands: Simian Aides for the Disabled are on the fourth floor of an office building on Commonwealth Avenue in Boston. On my first visit there I could hear monkeys chattering in the training room. I was eager to watch the training, but before that I wanted to talk to Mary Joan Willard, the educational psychologist who started and is director of Helping Hands.

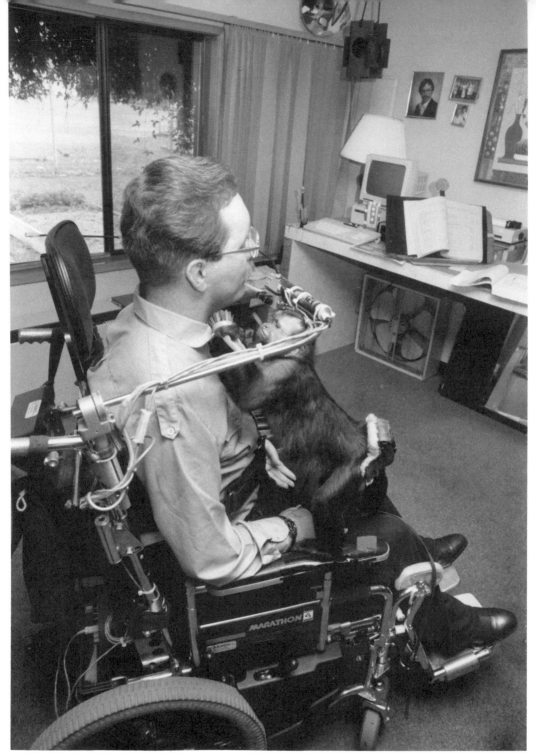

Peepers soothes Mitch's itching neck.

Quantum leaps of the imagination have always fascinated me, and I opened our conversation on that point. "How did you get the idea that monkeys might be trained to do things for paralyzed human beings?" I asked. "What made you think it was possible?"

Mary Joan explained that after receiving her doctorate in educational psychology from Boston University, she began a postdoctoral fellowship in 1977 at Tufts New England Medical Center in Boston. The fellowship was for rehabilitative study and work with persons who had suffered severe physical injury. In her daily rounds she soon came to know Joe, a patient at the center. One minute he had been a happy, healthy twenty-three year old. The next minute, because of a diving accident, he was a quadriplegic, paralyzed from the neck down. His story was an all-too-familiar one, but he was the first quadriplegic Mary Joan had ever known.

"I was shocked," she said. "I found it inconceivable that someone so young, so full of life was going to spend the rest of his days completely dependent on other people, dependent for a drink of water, for a bite of food, dependent on someone to bring him a book or turn out a light. I am a psychologist, and I kept thinking, There has to be some way to make him more independent.

"I couldn't get him out of my mind. I would sit in my room and think about him lying there in his room, helpless. And then one night it hit me out of the blue. Chimps! Why couldn't chimpanzees be trained to do things for quadriplegics like Joe? I kept thinking about it, and I didn't get much sleep that night."

The next day Mary Joan went to see B. F. Skinner, the famous Harvard psychologist who has done extensive pioneering research with animals, using reward and punishment techniques to alter their behavior. Mary Joan had worked three years for Skinner as a parttime assistant. He might not think her idea was workable, but she knew he would not scoff at it.

Skinner was amused at his assistant's excitement over her new idea; he pointed out that chimpanzees grow to be almost as big as humans, are stronger than humans, and often are bad-tempered. Chimpanzees would

Mary Joan Willard and a capuchin friend.

be too risky. But Mary Joan was right; Skinner did not laugh. The idea intrigued him.

Why not, he asked, think about using capuchins, the little creatures traditionally known as organ-grinder monkeys? They are small, usually no more than six or seven pounds and seldom more than eighteen inches tall. They are intelligent, easy to train, and form strong bonds of loyalty to their human masters. Furthermore, they have a long life expectancy, an average of about thirty years.

That was all the encouragement Mary Joan needed. She did some reading about capuchins, found out where they could be purchased, then went to the director of postdoctoral programs at Tufts and asked for money to start an experimental capuchin training program.

"He nearly fell off his chair laughing," Mary Joan said, remembering the director's first reaction to her proposal.

But Mary Joan was persistent and persuasive. When the director stopped laughing, he came through with a grant and some training space. The grant was just two thousand dollars, but it was enough for Mary Joan to buy four monkeys, some cages, and hire student trainers at one dollar an hour.

"I thought we could train them in eight weeks," Mary Joan recalled. "I had never touched a monkey! It took us eight weeks just to coax them out of their cages. The monkeys I was able to buy had had some pretty hard treatment. They weren't in a mood to trust any human being."

But a beginning had been made, and patience and dedication paid off in training the monkeys in an astonishing variety of tasks: taking food from a refrigerator and putting it in a microwave oven; turning lights on and off; doing the same with a television set, stereo, heater, air condi-tioner; opening and closing curtains; setting up books, magazines, and computer printouts on a reading stand.

One piece of equipment essential to most quadriplegics is a mouth-stick which is used for turning pages, dialing a phone, typing, working a computer, and many other actions which improve the quality of a quadri-plegic's life. One problem is that the mouthstick often falls to the floor or onto the wheelchair tray. The monkey helper is quickly taught to pick up the stick and replace it correctly in its master's mouth.

"The capuchins have great manual dexterity, greater than a human adult's," Mary Joan said, "and they're very bright. But we don't try to train them to do tasks where they have to think."

Judi Zazula, an occupational therapist, has been with Helping Hands almost from the beginning. Her title is program director, but Mary Joan describes her as a partner. Judi makes the same point about not putting a monkey in a situation where it has to think about the right way to do something. "Everything," she says, "is planned so that the monkey has just one way to respond if it does the task right."

The basic motivation for a monkey to perform a task correctly is a simple reward system. When it carries out a command as it is supposed to—turning on a VCR or bringing a drink—the trainer, and later the quadriplegic owner, praises the monkey for doing a good job and at the same time gives it a treat, usually a few drops of strawberry-flavored syrup. The quadriplegic releases the syrup by means of a wheelchair control.

There is also a system of punishment because capuchins are endlessly curious and occasionally mischievous. One monkey, for example, began dimming the lights when its owner was reading so that it would get a reward when it was told to turn them up again. More often, however, misbehavior is likely to be opening a drawer without being asked to or throwing paper out of a wastebasket in the hope of finding something interesting.

The monkeys are taught that anything with a white circular sticker pasted on it—such as a medicine cabinet—is off limits. If a monkey violates the off-limits rule, it is warned with a buzz from a small battery-operated device that it wears on a belt around its waist. If it doesn't obey the warning, the quadriplegic master can use remote controls to give the monkey a tiny electric shock. The warning buzz is usually sufficient, and most owners report that they almost never have to use the shock treatment. Judi Zazula points out that buzz-shock collars are also used in dog training.

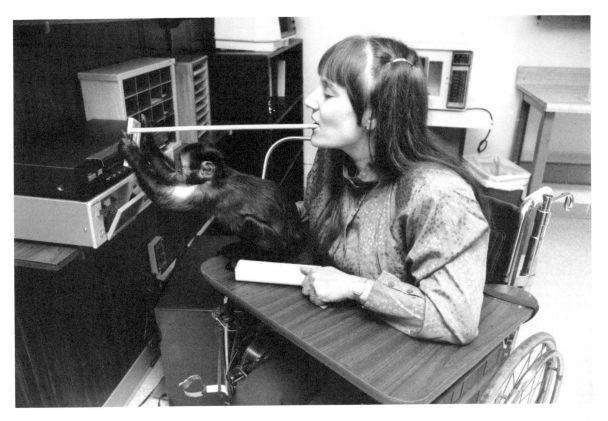

Judi Zazula teaches one of her bright pupils to place a tape in a cassette player.

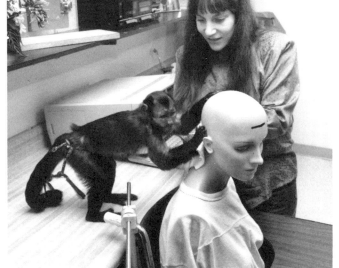

Practice makes perfect. Someday this monkey will gently rub a quadriplegic's itching nose or cheek.

LATE IN 1979 Robert Foster, a twenty-five-year-old quadriplegic living near Boston, became the first person to take part in a pilot project to test the feasibility of using a capuchin monkey aide. Robert, paralyzed from the shoulders down as the result of an automobile accident at the age of eighteen, had been living by himself for several years with the help of a personal care attendant. The attendant lived in the apartment with Robert but worked full time in a nearby hospital. That meant that Robert was alone in the apartment for nine hours or more at least five days a week.

Robert's new helper, a six-pound capuchin female named Hellion, helped to fill the long hours and continues to do so eight years after the experiment began. Robert communicates with Hellion—who deserves a nicer name—by aiming a small laser pointer at what he wants the monkey to bring or do. The laser is mounted on the chin control mechanism of his wheelchair. He also gives her a voice command such as "Bring" or "Open."

Hellion feeds Robert, brushes his hair, tidies up his wheelchair tray, brings him books, and carries out a whole range of other helpful tasks. For his part Robert dispenses strawberry-syrup rewards and tells Hellion how nice she is. Hellion is close by Robert's wheelchair all day, but when he tells her it is time for bed, she will go into her cage and lock the door.

As publicity about simian aides has spread across the country, Helping Hands has been swamped with requests for monkeys. Mary Joan and Judi are proceeding slowly with placements, however, still treating each case as an experiment. A number of additional capuchins have been placed with quadriplegics, and there have been no failures.

Mary Joan has had to spend an increasing amount of her time in fund raising and in administrative details of making Helping Hands a smoothly functioning nonprofit organization. "For the first two years we had to get along on three thousand dollars a year," Mary Joan said. "Fortunately, we don't have to pay student trainers much, and they love the experience."

Several major organizations and agencies concerned with severely disabled persons were interested, but all were skeptical. In the early stages Mary Joan wrote thirty-nine grant proposals and sent them to philanthropic foundations and government agencies, but not one was approved. But she persisted and, as evidence mounted that the capuchins could do the job, a trickle of financial support began. Now the Veterans Administration, National Medical Enterprises, the Educational Foundation of America, and the Paralyzed Veterans of America give some financial help to Helping Hands. Money is also received through private contributions, but fund raising still requires time that Mary Joan would rather be giving to other parts of the program.

Lack of money was not the only problem in the early days of the program. Some critics said that the idea of monkeys serving as helpers was demeaning to the quadriplegics as human beings. Some medical authorities said that mechanical equipment—robotics is the technical term—could be developed to do a better job than monkeys.

To the first criticism, Mary Joan points out that no one thinks it is beneath the dignity of a blind person to have a dog serve as a guide. As to robotic equipment, she agrees that for some quadriplegics mechanical tools may be best. But she points out that no piece of equipment can provide the companionship and sheer pleasure that an affectionate capuchin can.

"A robot won't sit in your lap and put its arms around you," Mary Joan said.

Developing a reliable supply of trainable monkeys was a problem that Helping Hands solved through the cooperation of Walt Disney World in Florida. A capuchin breeding colony has been established on Discovery Island in this world-famous recreational-educational center, and it will produce most of the monkeys needed in the quadriplegic program. Other monkeys are received through private donation, and Helping Hands has become a safe haven for monkeys that have been confiscated by government agencies because of mistreatment or having been brought into the country illegally.

Trial-and-error testing proved to the Helping Hands crew that early socialization was necessary to train a monkey that would be affectionate and happy when it became part of a human household. The answer has been the creation of a foster home program. When the monkeys from

Walt Disney World are young babies, six to eight weeks old, they are placed with foster families. These volunteer families agree to raise the monkeys in their homes for about three years and then turn them over to Helping Hands to be trained as aides to quadriplegics.

The carefully selected volunteer families agree to spend ten hours a day with their primate babies for the first six months—ten hours with the monkey outside its cage. This means that the foster mother and father and older children are actually carrying the baby monkey as they go about their household routines. Older monkeys require less time, but members of the household still must spend at least four hours daily with the young capuchin if it is to become a truly "humanized" primate.

Being a foster parent to a young monkey may sound like fun, and in many ways it can be a delightful experience. But it is time-consuming and demanding, and the time inevitably comes when the monkey must be given over to Helping Hands. "Everyone knows this moment of parting is coming, and most people handle it well," Mary Joan said, "but for some it is very hard. We have been offered as much as five thousand dollars to let a family keep a monkey. But, of course, we can't do that."

If for any reason a monkey does not successfully complete its training at Helping Hands, it is offered to its foster care family as a pet. Should the foster care family be unable to take it, Helping Hands maintains a carefully screened list of other families who have applied for a monkey pet. The "unsuccessful" monkey will be placed in the kind of human home environment to which it is accustomed.

Over sixty-five monkeys are now living with foster families. More than a hundred additional families have passed the screening test and are waiting to receive their foster "children."

Judi Zazula is a rehabilitation engineer. Together with Doug Ely, a solar research specialist for Arthur D. Little, Inc., she has designed most of the special equipment needed in the Helping Hands program: the laser pointer, chin and other wheelchair controls, and equipment that the capuchin's tiny hands can hold and manipulate.

"One of the first things I was asked to design was the nose scratcher,"

Judi told me and added, "The monkeys helped design a lot of the equipment."

She explained that by watching the monkeys as they carried out their tasks, she and Doug Ely could tell when a piece of equipment needed changing or when some new device was necessary.

Almost all of the monkeys selected for training are females because they tend to be gentler and more affectionate than males. Even so, to preclude the possibility of a capuchin aide hurting anyone, the teeth are extracted from the trainee monkeys when they reach maturity at about three-and-a-half to four years.

This operation has no harmful effects on the monkey or on her ability to eat and digest her food. All Helping Hands monkeys, from soon after they go into foster care, have a diet which is 85 percent commercial monkey food (Purina Monkey Chow). After teeth extraction the food pellets are softened a bit with water, and the monkey can eat them with no difficulty. The rest of the diet usually is fruit—bananas, apple slices, peaches—which the monkey, even without teeth, can eat easily, especially as her gums harden.

The training of a monkey usually takes about eight months. A session with the student trainer may last from half an hour to an hour, but it might be as short as ten minutes depending upon the monkey's personality. There may be several training sessions a day.

"Every monkey is different," Judi said. "Every one has her own personality and her own strengths and weaknesses."

Judi's biggest job within Helping Hands is to match the right monkey with the right quadriplegic who is being considered to receive one. A training log is kept on each monkey, and Judi pours over every page until she knows everything that can be known about a particular capuchin's personality and about her strengths and weaknesses.

Then Judi visits the quadriplegic. She stays at least two days and gets to know as much about the person as she can and about the environment where the monkey is going to live and work for the rest of her life. Judi even makes a video of the quadriplegic's living quarters so that they can be

Judi Zazula studying the record of one of the monkeys in training.

duplicated in the final training of the monkey the quadriplegic will receive.

"I am totally consumed with getting the right monkey in the right place," Judi said to me. "By the time they leave this training room, they are my children. I always think, what kind of life will they have out there? I want to make sure it will be the best and most useful life possible."

Judi has come to know dozens of quadriplegics very well, and she has thought a great deal about the total loss of hope that they suffer. "A spinal cord injury is an especially terrible thing," Judi said, "because it usually happens to young people, and it usually occurs at a happy moment in life—a car accident after a junior-senior prom or having fun diving into a swimming pool or playing football. Then everything is lost in a split second. The person comes to and his or her world has collapsed and a nightmare begins.

"Most people thinking about something like that happening to them say, 'I wouldn't want to live; I'd rather be dead.' But these people aren't dead. Slowly, if they begin to believe that they can do things and affect things, they begin to think that it is worth hanging around."

Both Mary Joan and Judi know very well that the success of Helping Hands depends upon how effective simian aides are in performing tasks that help quadriplegics lead better and more productive lives. But they also believe passionately that having a capuchin helper adds an interest and spice to quadriplegics' lives that can make a huge psychological difference. The companionship is important, but beyond that their ability to control the monkey makes them special. They can do something few other people can do.

As part of her master's degree work, Judi made a study of how people react to a quadriplegic with and without a monkey helper. When one quadriplegic she was using in her study was at a shopping center without his monkey, only two strangers stopped to talk with him in the course of an hour. When the monkey was sitting beside him on the wheelchair, seventy-one people took time from their shopping to speak to the quadriplegic during about the same amount of time.

"The quadriplegic who can control a monkey is an expert in a very unusual way," Judi said, "and that makes him interesting to other people."

One quadriplegic had this to say: "When I go outdoors in my wheelchair, all that people see is the wheelchair. But when I go out with my monkey, the only thing they see is the monkey. Nobody notices the chair at all."

Mary Joan Willard has a sense of history and a vision of the future. In terms of need and demand, Helping Hands may seem slow in getting trained monkeys to the thousands of quadriplegics who want them. But she points out that the possibility of training dogs to guide the blind had been debated and advocated for a century before the Seeing Eye program began early in this century.

"Compared to that, we are doing all right," Mary Joan said to me.

Mary Joan's immediate goal for Helping Hands is to place forty simian aides a year and to move beyond that as fast as the job can be done properly. Costs for training, equipment, and placement are approximately nine thousand dollars for each Helping Hands monkey. If a recipient is able to meet these costs from insurance payments or other personal resources, he or she is expected to do so; however, no one selected to receive a monkey is refused for inability to pay. For most quadriplegics, costs are met from U.S. Veterans Administration and state rehabilitation program funds or from private research or charitable organizations.

Of one thing Mary Joan Willard is sure. "I see this as a life's work," she told me.

Judi Zazula feels the same way. "I can't imagine getting the satisfaction out of anything else that I get from this work," she said.

Judi was recently married to Doug Ely, her long-time partner in equipment development. Instead of a flower girl, Judi decided to have a flower primate. Hellion, the first monkey to become a simian aide in the Helping Hands program, carried a little bouquet of flowers.

"When I Go to the Cemetery, My Job Will Be Over"

MARGARET GALLIMORE was waiting for us on the porch of her house on Birmingham Street. The house, once white but now a faded noncolor, is located in a poor, black, depressed area near downtown Dallas. Her house, like most of those in the neighborhood, is of substantial size.

"Is this Mathis Hospice?" Paul asked, looking doubtful.

Mrs. Gallimore laughed. "That's Mathis Hospice," she said, pointing to the house next door, which was roughly a twin of her own. "Come on and meet some of my guys."

In the hospice living room were two men watching television. Even without the knowledge that Mathis Hospice is a home for AIDS victims, we would have known that these men were ill, very, very ill. We sat down and talked to them. Bryan, a thirty-year-old white, was tall, pale, thin, totally without energy. He had been living at the hospice for three weeks. Before the ravages of AIDS he had been a printer, a good one he said with a touch of pride. Now he was too drained to work.

"Standing for a long time is very hard for me," he said. He looked around the clean, neat, but spartanly furnished living room. "This hospice is a haven for me. I was living in a crummy, roach-infested apartment that the owner made me leave."

Bryan is a drug-using alcoholic; he is getting therapy from Alcoholics Anonymous and Drugs Anonymous.

Raymond, thirty-one, a black alcoholic, had a particularly sad story to tell. He went to Boston earlier in the year and fell in love with a woman who had five children. "I loved them like my own," he said. "I was going to marry her this Christmas."

But he shared a needle with her one night and then discovered that she had AIDS. She died late in August. In Raymond's case there was no long incubation period as there sometimes is with AIDS. Only two months later, in mid-autumn, he learned that he had the deadly disease and returned to Dallas, where he had been born and raised. He intended to live with his mother, but when her landlord found out that Raymond had AIDS, he threatened to evict her. Raymond went to a homeless shelter, but when his condition became known, he was put out on the street. At that point he was without money, living under bridges, unable to keep clean or warm. Then he heard about Mathis Hospice and went there. Margaret Gallimore took him in.

"I'm thankful to have a place to lay my head and somebody who cares and understands," Raymond said. "It's so hard to keep being turned away. We become outcasts. Nobody wants us around. They want to put us in a pen away from society. You have this disease and nobody wants you around. This is what I want—this hospice—where I can have clean clothes, a good meal, a bath, be out of the cold." And then he said again, "Somebody to care and understand."

Margaret Gallimore cares and understands. She has been a private duty nurse for more than twenty years, and she knows suffering. Mrs. Gallimore, who is forty-four, was born in Dallas and spent her girlhood there; after that she lived in New York and California, practicing nursing and raising her family of two boys and a girl. Then she returned to Dallas in 1984 to take care of an aunt who was dying of cancer.

"Aunt Mathis," Mrs. Gallimore told us. "She had no family of her

Margaret Gallimore and hospice resident.

own, so my children and I were her family. She lived with us some of the years in New York and California."

While she was nursing her aunt, Mrs. Gallimore became increasingly aware of a need in the area for a place for homeless people to live. When her aunt died, Mrs. Gallimore rented the house next door and turned it into a shelter for homeless men. That was in 1986, and she took in over two hundred men over a period of months who otherwise would have slept on the streets.

Then one night she saw on an evening newscast that an AIDS clinic was closing because no one wanted to work there. She heard that AIDS victims were losing their jobs and homes and couldn't find places to live. "So I said, 'I have a place,'" Mrs. Gallimore recalls. "'They can stay here.'"

Mrs. Gallimore turned the homeless shelter into an AIDS hospice and called it Mathis Hospice in memory of her aunt. "I fixed it up," she told us. "I'm still fixing it up. I'd work for a week and buy a bed, another week and get a ceiling fan. When necessary, I'd use my savings. Once I needed to get my car out of the repair garage, but there were three men dying at the hospice, and I needed things to make them a little more comfortable. So I let the car stay in the garage and used the bus."

Thirty-two PWAs, which is what Mrs. Gallimore calls people with AIDS, have stayed at Mathis Hospice since she took the first person in. Fifteen have died. "I'm sad a lot of the time," she said. "It is hard to lose one. But it doesn't make me want to stop. I have decided to devote my life to caring for AIDS victims because so many times their families turn them away, and their friends walk away from them.

"I hope science finds a cure and puts me out of AIDS work. But if it does, I'll still be taking care of someone—the homeless, the elderly. They'll be around forever."

"Won't the time come when you say, 'I've done enough?'" Paul asked.

"When I go to the cemetery, my job will be over," Mrs. Gallimore said.

Where does her motivation come from? What made her the way she is? I asked Mrs. Gallimore those questions, and she said, "It's God-given. The good Lord made me this way. I can't stand to see people suffer. I can't stand to see dogs and cats suffer."

Once Mrs. Gallimore told the *Dallas Times Herald:* "As a kid I wanted to be a missionary and take the faith to foreign lands. They tell me I'm doing my missionary work now. I've been their father, their mother, and their brother. I bathe them when they are dying. I feed them."

From the very beginning Mrs. Gallimore made the decision that she would put no restriction on the kind of AIDS patients she would take care of in Mathis Hospice. As a result she gets some of the most difficult cases. There is but one apartment in the area that will accept people with AIDS and only then if they are "ambulatory"—can still walk. Mathis Hospice will take those who are bedridden and must have everything done for them. One man with AIDS could find no place to live because doctors believed that he had no more than a month to live. Mrs. Gallimore took him in and nursed him day and night. He lived seven months. Another young AIDS sufferer was turned away from every facility because he was a convicted arsonist. Mathis Hospice accepted him.

"We're a family at Mathis Hospice," Mrs. Gallimore said. "I do the cooking and clean house. I nurse them and give them baths. I take them for rides in my car so they can have a change of scene and get some fresh air."

Finances for the hospice are always a problem. One friend contributes five hundred dollars a month regularly. Otherwise Mrs. Gallimore supports the cost of running the hospice—food, rent, utilities, beds and linens, and all the rest—through her work as a nurse, taking just enough assignments to raise the cash necessary to meet expenses.

"I'm not gone from the hospice any longer than I have to," she said.

"Why don't you ask the city and charity organizations to help?" I asked.

"I just got tired of begging," she said.

Mrs. Gallimore gets help from her two teenage sons, Philip Ray and Willie James. They do heavy chores around the hospice and turn heavy patients in bed. Mrs. Gallimore also receives a great deal of help from her daughter, Pamela, when Pamela is at home. She is studying nursing at a college near Dallas, and is now at home only on holidays and during summer vacation.

But Pamela wants to take over the running of Mathis Hospice when she graduates, so that her mother can start hospices in other cities. "So that not so many people with AIDS will have to leave their home towns to find a place where they can get help," Mrs. Gallimore said.

"Do you have cities in mind?" I asked.

"Washington, D.C., for one," she said. "I've already been asked to start an AIDS hospice there."

Mrs. Gallimore made a trip to the nation's capital recently. On one of the hospice walls is a photograph of her with two of the people she met there: President and Mrs. Reagan. She was called to Washington to receive one of the President's Volunteer Action Awards for 1988, one of the eighteen people from all over the United States to be so honored. The award is considered to be the most prestigious that can be received for volunteer service.

Mrs. Gallimore does not hide her pleasure at receiving this very special honor. But when we talked about it, she said, "They put me up in this big, expensive hotel. My, that money could have been used to help people with AIDS."

2

Making a Difference in the Environment

Ila at one of her twice-weekly turtle shows.

A Love Affair with Turtles

SHE IS a tiny, wire-thin, bouncy woman with lovely white hair and a face deeply lined from eighty-three years of life, much of it spent in the sun, wind, and sea of the Texas Gulf Coast. Her name is Ila Marie Fox Loetscher, but throughout Texas and over much of the rest of the country she is known simply as the "Turtle Lady."

For more than a quarter of a century Ila Loetscher has lived in her beach home on South Padre Island, Texas, and carried out an educational campaign and program to save sea turtles, which are now endangered species of reptiles. At present rates of loss some of these ancient sea creatures may become extinct before the end of this century. But not if Ila can help it.

For a long time, though, sea turtles had no part in her life. She was born in Iowa in 1904, far from the sea, and graduated from the University of Iowa in 1927. One of her early passions was aviation. She was the first woman to be issued a private pilot's license in Iowa. She became a charter member of the International Womens Pilot Association; the group, still known as the 99s, was made up of the first ninety-nine women pilots in the world. Amelia Earhart was one of Ila's friends. In 1935 Ila married David Loetscher, a chemical engineer, and they made their home in New Jersey.

After her husband's death in 1959, Ila moved to South Padre Island and built one of the first permanent homes on the sandy shore of the Gulf of Mexico in that area. And just as she was a pioneer in aviation, she became a pioneer in the protection of sea turtles. Her beginning was a modest one. She found an injured Atlantic ridley sea turtle, named it Geraldine, and nursed it back to health.

Injured sea turtles were struggling out of the Gulf onto South Padre Island all the time, Ila discovered. She began to take care of them. Her neighbors learned about her concern and brought her sick or wounded sea turtles that they found. Ila made tanks and pools for them in the yard around her house so that they would have a place to get well. If a turtle recovered sufficiently, it would be released back to the sea. If it couldn't survive in the Gulf, it became one of Ila's permanent residents.

Some people thought it strange that Ila spent so much of her time worrying about sea turtles. "Those people just didn't understand how intelligent sea turtles are and how much they need our help," Ila explains.

Little by little Ila found out a great deal about sea turtles. There had been a time, she learned, when millions of the great sea reptiles made their home in the Gulf of Mexico. But they were a big business in Central America and Mexico then. Fishermen and businessmen killed them by the hundreds of thousands. They were prized for their meat, their eggs, their leather to make boots, their oil to make cosmetics, their shells to make combs and other tourist items.

Some of the facts that Ila learned were appalling. Slaughterhouses on Mexico's Pacific coast processed as much as sixty thousand pounds of turtle meat a day during the catching season. Sometimes as many as 120,000 Pacific ridley turtles would clamber onto a beach in one night. Men with wagons would simply scoop them up and carry them away. Sea turtles are still hunted commercially, though, because of their growing scarcity, the business is not nearly as large as it once was.

The tragic depletion can be told in one example. In 1947 naturalists

Ila never gets tired of talking about turtles.

counted 47,000 Kemp's ridley sea turtles coming ashore in one day on a beach called Rancho Nuevo on Mexico's northern Gulf coast. In 1988 not more than five hundred Kemp's ridleys have come onto this beach during the entire nesting season. The Kemp's ridley and other species of sea turtles are in grave danger of disappearing from the sea and from the earth. They will go the way of the dinosaur if their slaughter is not stopped.

In 1978 Ila Loetscher founded Sea Turtle, Incorporated, using the downstairs part of her home as the office. Her idea was to build a nonprofit organization that would sponsor educational programs about sea turtles through the schools, tourist bureaus, civic clubs, television, radio, newspapers, and magazines. And that is what Ila and several volunteer helpers have been doing for the past ten years: telling the world about sea turtles and about the grave danger they are in. Ila personally visits schools throughout Texas, talking with thousands of students about turtles.

And at her home on South Padre Island, Ila puts on two "Meet the Turtles" shows—one on Tuesday, one on Saturday—every week of the year. More than ten thousand people from all over the United States attend these shows each year and learn about sea turtles.

The shows take place in a small open-air theater where people can sit on wooden benches. Next to the benches are several large tanks in which various kinds of turtles swim. The morning we visited the show, one of Ila's volunteer helpers warned the crowd—mainly families with children—not to dangle their fingers over the edge of the tank while they were watching the turtles. "Turtles have poor eyesight, and they will think your fingers are shrimp," she explained.

And then Ila came out and stood on a platform in front of the audience, full of energy, smiling, so obviously in love with her turtles. She carried Jerry, an Atlantic green turtle dressed in a red dress and wig. Jerry has a masculine name because Ila names her turtles for the people who bring them to her. Like all the turtles in residence, Jerry had been injured when someone had tied a string to one of her flippers. The injury had never healed properly, and Jerry is one of the permanent boarders.

Ila's talk was full of information about turtles. "Sea turtles are territorial. They return to their birthplaces. Sometimes it takes twenty-seven years, but they always return. We don't understand how they always find the place where they were born. Maybe it's a question of scent."

Ila removed Jerry's dress. "Jerry has 139 years to live—a long time to have fun. Let's show how beautiful she is when she skinny-dips." The information keeps coming. "Turtles can stay underwater for fifteen minutes. They have great ears, but their eyes are their weakest part."

Ila treats her turtles like children, calling them "sweetheart" and saying things like, "Do that for Mama." She tells the crowd a horror story of a Mexican businessman who boils sea turtles alive for their oil, which goes into cosmetics. A groan goes up from the audience.

"Turtles love each other just as we love our fellow man," Ila said, telling a story of how two of her resident turtles supported an injured newcomer who was unable to float.

Another volunteer, M. L. "Doc" Hall, came out with a huge, wildly flapping loggerhead named Blunderbuss. It was much too large for Ila to cope with so Doc held it while she talked about it. Blunderbuss weighed only half an ounce when he arrived at Ila's home with a fisherman's line wrapped around him.

The third turtle in the show was Tex, a hawksbill, which wore a small hat. He had been blind from birth. Ila gave him several kisses. "He's a sweet little fellow, and we all love him," she said. Another hawksbill named Pancho joined the show. The hawksbill is an endangered species and is the favorite raw material of people who deal in tortoiseshell trinkets. Ila tells how young hawksbills swim "lickety-split" out to sea three days after birth until they can reach the shelter of rocks.

Ila has taught Pancho a simple trick. "Now put your head down on Mama's hand," she tells the turtle, and he does just that.

Later we talked to Schatzie Smith, a teacher on South Padre Island who is another one of Ila's volunteer helpers. "After you hang out with Ila, you don't have any doubt why you're here," she said. "Somehow the injured turtles that arrive here know right away that she is their friend. She handles them so much she smells like a turtle! That hawksbill, Tex,

Ila looks on as volunteer M. L. "Doc" Hall displays a loggerhead named Blunderbuss.

came here with a reputation of being a biter, but Ila had him in the show within three days. Ila has a lot of energy and strength, but she tells us that if it wasn't for the turtles she wouldn't be here. They sustain her and keep her going."

Ila puts it very clearly. "The purpose of our program is to save sea turtles," she said. "Anything that is as harmless as a sea turtle should not be destroyed. They are my friends. Once they discover that you are their friend, they will never do anything to harm you. The purpose of our work and programs is to spread the word."

The word certainly is spreading. Largely because of Ila's program, the Mexican government has started to cooperate in the protection of some species of sea turtles. And a U.S. government program is working to start new protected nesting areas on the Texas Gulf Coast. Recently the National Wildlife Federation honored Ila Loetscher with a Special Conservation Achievement Award.

The award pleased Ila, but always it is her turtles that are on her mind. "Every morning when I get up," she told Paul and me, "I go out on my balcony and call down to my turtles. They can't see me, but they can hear me. 'Where is that old woman?' they say. So I go down where they can see me."

The Seventy-Nine-Mile Dream

SEVENTY-NINE miles does not seem far in an age when an automobile can cover that distance in an hour and an airplane in a few minutes. But it is a long, long way when every one of those seventy-nine miles winds along a river and is covered by brush and fallen trees that must be hacked out by ax or cut out by handsaw.

Jack Glover knows how far it is. Since 1973, he has been working to restore an old trail along the North Umpqua River in southwestern Oregon, a trail that was traveled by Indians and pioneers in the last century but which has disappeared from lack of use and has been taken back by nature. When reclamation is complete, this trail that winds through the Umpqua National Forest will provide a hiking trail that connects with the Pacific Crest National Scenic Trail. This great trail extends from the Canadian border to the Mexican border.

Forest Service officials originally thought that work on the North Umpqua River trail would not be completed until the year 2000. But Jack Glover has been so successful in encouraging volunteer groups to work on the trail that completion in 1991 now seems likely.

"That's a better date," Jack says with a smile. Born in 1915, he is now seventy-four.

Jack lives to downplay his own work on the trail and emphasize that local chapters of the Boy Scouts, Audubon Society, Izaak Walton League, and other organizations have worked hard to advance the trail. But officials of the Forest Service and Bureau of Land Management are well aware of Jack's contribution to the trail.

"You can go up there in the middle of the week in the winter—when it's cold—and you'll find him out there working alone," says Larry Lee of the Bureau of Land Management. "And then he leads volunteers out there on the weekend. The trail wouldn't exist without him."

If there was ever a labor of love, the North Umpqua River trail is exactly that for Jack Glover. Before his retirement, Jack was a graphic artist in the local school system, preparing instructional materials. While the main value of the North Umpqua River trail may always be for recreation, he also sees it as an important instructional tool in the natural sciences for school groups, Scouts, and others. And for himself, an outdoorsman and naturalist, work on the trail is perfect at his present time of life. "For a retirement activity it's a treat," he says. "There's a great heritage of fresh air and forest, and the North Umpqua River is the jewel in this setting."

The day we went to the trail with him, Jack threw an armload of construction tools—things with strange names like sanvik, pulaski, fire rake—into the back of his battered old green Ford station wagon. He talked as we drove. "The back country is very refreshing, particularly for anybody who feels the stress of city life. A principal motivation of my work has been to make back country more accessible and share it with others. We need to substitute some other form of recreation for motorized recreation. The bottom line is to get people out of their cars and using their legs again."

The road started paralleling the North Umpqua River, which was a vivid green, truly a jewel. Jack is an ardent fly fisherman. "That river is filled with lunkers," he said. "I've done a lot of fishing there. I used to wear a hole in the road and never had any time for recreation for myself. I felt

Jack Glover at work on the North Umpqua River Trail.

In 1987, Jack Glover received the President's Volunteer Action Award for his work on the North Umpqua River Trail.

Photographs by David Conklin.

like I couldn't let the work slack off for even a little while. I was afraid I would lose all my volunteers, afraid they would wander off. I think cars are a modern curse, but my friends used to kid me that I'm one of the worst offenders because I was driving back and forth so much."

We parked. Jack changed into his hiking boots and put a small ax into a backpack. He carried the fire rake and pulaski. "This is my trail-building kit," he said.

We struck off through the woods, and immediately the naturalist in him came out in a steady stream of comments:

"There's a pileated woodpecker living in that snag over there."

He pointed to an area of fallen tree trunks. "This is a blowdown. Wind and snow combined to create this mess."

Of a pile of animal droppings in the middle of the trail: "That's a bear."

The woods became so dense that sunlight hardly filtered through. We had a sense that things had changed very little from the days that this forest was home only to Indians. The trees were festooned with moss, an indication of the great amount of rainfall here in the southern Cascades. Jack was a fast walker. We had to struggle to keep up with him. Along the way he pointed out where he had put in drainage systems to keep the trail from being washed away. Once he stopped to chop out a stump that was blocking the trail.

Jack Glover has spent many, many days out on the trail. He estimates that he has worked on it at least five thousand hours. But after he finished with the stump, he rested a bit, and it was clear that he wasn't thinking of the huge amount of labor he had put in on the trail.

"I've had lots of fun out here," he said.

Outwitting Señor Coyote

THAT RATHER grim bumper sticker on the pickup ahead of us seemed to give added point to our trip that day to the Jornada Experimental Range near Las Cruces, New Mexico. The purpose of our visit was to talk with Dr. Dean M. Anderson about sheep and goat losses to coyote predators and to look at an experiment he was running to combat the problem.

Stock losses to predators is not the number one problem of ranchers in this part of the American Southwest. That dubious distinction belongs to years of recurring drought and to the steady encroachment of mesquite, tarbush, and creosote bush into the grasslands, an encroachment that threatens to turn the already arid country into a desert.

But predators are a relentless enemy that can make the difference between a profitable year and a losing one. The predators may be big cats or even bears that come down from the mountains to prey on domestic livestock; they may be golden eagles, which can snatch young lambs and goats. Most feared and despised, however, is the coyote, the wily old range villain that has plagued stockmen since the beginning of ranching.

61

They are deadly to calves that have strayed from their mothers and to sheep of any age.

Ranchers and sheepmen wage steady war on coyotes. They carry rifles in their pickups and blaze away at any coyote they see on their land. Poison is used, though less frequently now. Traps are used. Guard dogs are used. Electric fences will protect sheep in small pastures but are too expensive for flocks on the open range. When coyotes increase rapidly in an area, the government animal damage control unit is called in, and the coyotes are trapped or shot from helicopters.

But all these methods have technical, humanitarian, environmental, and legal problems, and are often too expensive. They can have momentary effectiveness, but they have not solved the coyote problem. No one knows how many coyotes roam the American West today. They are too mobile to make an estimate that would mean anything. Similarly, it is hard to get a picture of the total damage they do. One study in New Mexico showed a loss of twenty thousand lambs a year to coyotes "before docking" (that period before the lambs' tails are bobbed). One thing is certain: in the lore, legend, and literature of the Southwest, both Spanish and Indian, the coyote is a savvy creature, a trickster, with almost magic powers of survival.

DEAN M. ANDERSON is a man with the coyote's love for the taste of lamb very much on his mind. He is one of the senior animal research scientists at the Jornada Experimental Range. This huge federal government research area in southeastern New Mexico covers 193,000 acres and represents 40 percent of the Department of Agriculture's land holdings in the United States. Dean has worked at the experimental range ever since receiving his Ph.D. degree from Texas A. & M. University in 1977.

We met Dean in his office at the USDA Agricultural Research Service in Las Cruces and began talking immediately about the sheep protection research project that he and a scientist colleague, Dr. Clarence V. Hulet, have been working on for several years. The idea is perfectly simple, as good ideas so often are. It amounts to this: if sheep and cows can somehow be got to graze together on the open range—form a single group instead of a separate flock and herd—the cows might protect the sheep from coyote attacks.

Dean is a tall, slow-talking man who seems at ease in Stetson, Levi's, and boots as only a true Westerner can. He calls himself a country boy. "Coyotes love lamb," he said, as we sat in his office. "But cows hate canines—coyotes, dogs, any kind of canine. Those old cows will go for any coyote or dog that gets close to them or their calves. I was reading a research paper a few years ago when one line just jumped out and hit me. It said that when sheep and cattle were run together and stay together, predator losses were less.

"Okay. That would be fine in a small fenced pasture where they would be bunched up. But here in the West on open range or pastures that cover dozens of square miles, the cattle graze by themselves, and the sheep flocks go their own way. They seldom graze together. You can start them out together, and it won't be long before you'll have a herd of cows in one place and half a mile away a flock of sheep.

"Clarence and I talked about it. If we could find a way to keep cattle and sheep together while they grazed, the cows might protect the sheep from coyotes. It seemed too simple. Surely someone had tried it. We went through all the research literature, but there wasn't a thing. So we said, 'Let's try it.'"

That was in 1985. Dean and Hulet studied bonding experiments of sheep dogs and sheep and read the works of Konrad Lorenz, who won a Nobel Prize for his studies of group behavior and the ways that some animals and birds imprint on or become attached to others. Then they started their own experiments, which are still going on after three years.

"Come on," Dean said. "Let's go see the flerd."

"The flerd?" I repeated.

Dean grinned. "You won't find that word in the dictionary. Clarence made it up from flock and herd."

We climbed into Dean's pickup and drove to the Jornada Experimental Range. The range was pure Southwestern desert: long vistas against a background of stark, dramatic mountains. Dean continued to talk as he guided the pickup over the rough dirt tracks.

"Coyotes are getting bolder all the time," he said. "They're extending their range to where they're raiding flocks on farms that are near towns and cities. Here in range country coyote predation is probably the main reason that some sheep raisers go out of business. If you can't keep your animals alive, the bank forecloses on you. You can be sure of that."

Before we reached the cows and sheep, we came upon a group of eight camels grazing peacefully in a pasture. We knew about the camel experiment that Dean and his colleagues were embarked on, but it was still a surprise to see the single-humped dromedaries looking very much at home on the American range. We asked Dean to stop and tell us about the experiment.

The camels continued to graze as Dean approached them. They let him rub their necks, and one nuzzled him, obviously looking for a treat. "A year ago they were completely wild animals in central Australia," Dean said. "We leased them from an animal importer six months ago. They've settled in real fast.

"You know that controlling undesirable brush—mesquite, tarbush, creosote bush, broom smoke weed—and improving the conditions of the rangeland is our number one challenge. We try to kill mesquite and the other woody plants with chemicals or tear them out with bulldozers, but that is limited by environmental worries and expense. So we're trying to add a biological control facet to our undesirable plant control program. We know from earlier studies that 80 percent of a camel's diet can be made up of woody plants like the ones we're trying to get rid of. If we can turn some of those plants into usable protein—camel meat is supposed to be good and their hides are usable—that would be great. If we can make use of camels in an economically and ecologically sound way, then it's good science and good business."

"It will take a lot of camels to make much of a dent in this brush," Paul said.

"If it works, camels will be just one more weapon in the fight," Dean said. "We won't give up chemicals and mechanical means. And please

64

don't go back and write that we're going to try to get ranchers to give up cattle and start raising camels. We're not dunderheads. And the camels may not work. We are monitoring them and their diet closely, but answers will take time."

Finally, we reached our destination, a group of cows, sheep, and goats closely bunched and grazing on the open range. "There it is," Dean said, a note of satisfaction in his voice. "The flerd."

He told us that there were forty-seven sheep, twenty-nine cows, thirteen Spanish goats, sixteen Angora goats, and four Akbash, lean, white dogs from Turkey noted for their animal guarding ability.

"It looks simple, doesn't it," Dean said, "the cattle, sheep, and goats just moving along together? Believe me, it wasn't simple. We had to experiment endlessly; it would take me all day to give you details about all the combinations. But the basic idea was to put young lambs—45, 60, 90 days old, we tried different ages—with eight- to nine-month-old heifers and keep them in pen confinement for different lengths of time—thirty, sixty days. Some heifers wouldn't tolerate lambs; they would butt and kick them. But most would tolerate, and after the confinement, the sheep would follow any heifers which tolerated them. The bonding just works one way—the sheep follow cows, not the other way around.

"So it looked like bonding would work. Then we had to find out if bonding—having the sheep and cows together—cut down on coyote attacks on the bonded sheep. We ran a series of tests comparing the number of attacks on bonded sheep to unbonded ones in a similar environment. There were almost no coyote attacks on bonded sheep, but in some cases half the unbonded ones would be lost to coyote predation.

"We tried bonding Angora goats to heifers. At first they appeared to bond. However, the bond did not endure under pasture conditions. We don't know why. Then we tried the three together in the bonding process—heifers, sheep, and goats. That worked. Angora goats apparently bond to the sheep and follow the sheep when the sheep follow the cows. In contrast, it appears that Spanish goats bond directly to cattle."

Paul asked about the Akbash.

"Bonding by itself probably isn't enough," Dean said. "Guard dogs

Dean Anderson with part of the camel experiment. The dromedaries were imported to eat woody brush, but Anderson is concerned with their taste for good New Mexico grass.

A part of the flerd.

are important. But we knew from experience that dogs by themselves are not enough. They go off to eat. They chase a rabbit. They sleep. The answer may be bonding plus the guard dogs. We have lots of research and experimenting still to do. Lots of questions have yet to be answered: how long will the bonding last? What new problems will come up when we apply bonding to commercial herds and flocks?

"But we know this. These cows, sheep, goats, and dogs grew up together after weaning. They tolerate each other and move together, and the coyotes are staying away. This flerd works."

"What does it mean if it works on a big scale?" I asked.

"It means more sheepmen will stay in business," Dean said. "It means we wouldn't have to rely so much on lethal means of coyote control: guns, poison, traps. It means coyotes would spend more time hunting their natural prey—rabbits, other small animals, birds—and that would result in a better ecological balance."

The day was getting late, the sun low on a cool November day. In the distance I heard a coyote try out his first howl of the evening. The howl ended in a series of yips, and to me it sounded just a little bit like a laugh.

I looked at Dean, an experienced, able animal research scientist willing to search for unusual answers in this hard country where there are no easy answers. He was studying the flerd intently, still looking for things he could learn.

I heard the howl and yip again, and I thought, Mr. Coyote, if you're laughing, maybe you're making a mistake. Maybe you just don't know what's going on.

3

Making a Difference through Community Service

Ron Cowart at an Explorer Troop 68 meeting.

The Asian Odyssey
of Ron Cowart

RON COWART went to Vietnam in 1968 when he was nineteen. He was in the U.S. Navy, but he spent thirteen months in the Mekong Delta assigned to the Ninth Infantry Division. "I was a sheltered young man, and I saw things that kids my age should never have seen," Ron said. "I had never experienced death, but I found myself putting my friends into body bags, friends I'd been talking to only a few minutes before.

"I was eager to go to Vietnam—very idealistic—ready to fight the Communists. I had a chance to get to know the people, to eat with them in their villages. I slowly discovered that a lot of them hated us and wanted us to leave. I came back disillusioned, hating 'those people.'"

Ron was discharged in 1969, decorated with the Purple Heart for wounds received in battle and the Navy Achievement Medal with "Combat V" for valor. He returned to the Dallas-Fort Worth area where he had been born and raised, and he decided that he wanted to be a policeman. That had been a childhood dream, and he found that it was still very much alive. He went through the police academy and joined the Dallas Police Department that same year, 1969.

Ron was ambitious and full of energy, and he knew he wanted to move up the ladder in the police department. He enrolled in college, took an undergraduate degree in criminal justice and a master's degree in liberal arts. He earned both degrees in six years, all the while working full time as a policeman.

"I thought Vietnam was behind me," he said, "a closed chapter in my life."

But the chapter was far from closed. Vietnam was not finished as a part of his life. Instead, it was about to enter his life again in a very different way.

SINCE THE end of the Vietnam War over a million refugees from Vietnam, Cambodia, and Laos have come to America. Southeast Asians are now the third largest ethnic group in the United States, and thousands have made their way to every major American city. Dallas, with its warm climate, is no exception. The city's estimated Southeast Asian population now exceeds thirty-five thousand, with the heaviest concentration living in a one-square-mile area of East Dallas that has become known to Dallas residents as "Little Asia."

Almost the entire Asian population of this East Dallas enclave fled Vietnam, Cambodia, or Laos with little more than the clothes they wore. Most spent months or years in refugee camps in Thailand, Malaysia, or Indonesia. When they finally arrived in the United States, all were penniless, few were able to speak English, and even fewer had any knowledge of how to survive in this strange new land. They packed themselves into the dreary apartments of East Dallas because they could afford to live nowhere else.

In May, 1974, Ron Cowart was assigned to one of the Dallas Police Department special weapons tactical squads that respond to the most serious city emergencies. Between emergencies, these squads patrol high-crime areas of the inner city, mostly at night, and it was as a part of such patrols that Cowart had his first real look at Little Asia, the shabby streets, the rundown blocks of dreary brick apartments. He saw the poorly dressed Southeast Asians in numbers that he had never expected to see again.

"I saw them, but I kept them out of my mind," Ron said. "They were a part of my life that I didn't want to open up again."

Then one day he noticed a group of Vietnamese boys going into one of the apartments. "I couldn't explain it then, and I can't explain it now," Ron said, "but something about those kids—their faces, the way they laughed and talked in Vietnamese—took me right back to Vietnam. They were just like the kids I had seen over there, and for some reason I wanted to see how they were living inside that building. I followed them in, and I guess I've never been the same since.

"It was like stepping back in time. The hall was full of the smell of Vietnamese food cooking, a good smell, nothing else quite like it. It was a hot day, like a furnace in that building, and the apartment doors were open. I could hear Vietnamese music, or maybe it was Cambodian, and Asian languages up and down the hall. I could see into the apartments. Out on the street the men wear Western clothes. Here in their apartments they were wearing sarongs and sandals and squatting on the floor in groups, talking just like in a hut in Vietnam. That's where I was, back in Vietnam, and I felt something I never thought I would feel for that place or those people—nostalgia."

That was the beginning of an unusual mental and emotional odyssey for Ron Cowart. In the weeks and months ahead, he began occasionally to talk to Vietnamese, Cambodian, and Laotian kids on the street. He went back into the apartments now and then and talked to the men and women. Not that talking was easy. Ron was, after all, a policeman in uniform with a gun on his hip. Where these people had come from, police meant trouble and guns could mean death. The police were people you stayed away from and talked to as little as possible. But in time they saw that nothing bad happened when this policeman came around, and they did talk to him; little by little, he learned about them and about their problems.

But Ron's real learning and his real involvement with the people of Little Asia began in 1977 when he married. His wife, Melinda, was then, and is now, a teacher at Spence Middle School in East Dallas. Her subject is English as a Second Language, and her students are primarily Vietnamese, Cambodian, and Laotian children from Little Asia.

She told Ron about her students, about what she had learned of their perilous escapes from their countries, the nightmarish experiences on the open ocean in flimsy boats, the months of hunger and boredom in refugee camps, the problems of their parents trying to make a living in America. She told her husband about how polite her Asian students were, about how hard they studied and how smart many of them were.

Sometimes in the evenings Melinda would visit her students in their apartments and talk to their parents. Ron began to go along on these home visits, and he saw things he had not yet clearly seen: children hungry and malnourished, men who could find no work, fifteen people crowded into a one-bedroom apartment in order to save money.

"I had never seen such concentrated misery in my life," Ron said. "Those terrible apartments. No air conditioning, no heating, backed-up toilets, broken windows, broken doors. The most insensitive landlords I've ever come across. Crime everywhere. People had to lock themselves in their apartments—if their locks worked. The walls are paper thin. When Melinda and I would walk through those buildings at night, I could hear people crying. Vandals—gangs, really—used to break in and terrorize the people in the apartments. There was a lot of fear."

By this time Ron Cowart was sure he wanted to do something—he knew he was *going* to do something—to help the people of Little Asia. He was a policeman, and he was going to help through the police. But the problem was to get people over their fear of the police so that they would report crimes and suspicious activity, register their property, make complaints against landlords, and come to the police for other help. Part of the problem was language. How could you get people to report trouble if they couldn't speak English? Part of the problem was just the lingering distrust of anyone in uniform.

The answer, Ron decided, was in the kids that he had come to know much better through Melinda's work. With the blessings of the Dallas Police Department and the Boy Scouts of America, Ron organized Ex-

Ron Cowart and Public Service Officer Leck Keovilay visit a Little Asia family.

Explorer Troop 68 meeting at the storefront. The East Dallas Community Police and Refugee Affairs Center was named "Best Inner-City Crime Reduction Project in U.S." by Police Foundation, Washington, D.C., in 1987.

plorer Post 68, recruiting boys between the ages of fourteen and seventeen from the apartments of Little Asia. Their first meeting place was the Highland Baptist Church in East Dallas, and thirty boys soon joined. Explorer Post 68 was the first post in the country made up entirely of refugee youth from Cambodia, Laos, and Vietnam; it is to this day the only Explorer Post sponsored by a police department.

Ron was right. Explorer Post 68 proved to be the bridge to the parents and the Southeast Asian community. They felt parental and group pride at seeing their sons in the crisp, clean Explorer uniforms that Ron somehow found money for. The Explorers had fun, played games, went on field trips, but they also began to carry out important community service: installing more than three hundred peepholes in apartment doors, collecting food, blankets, and oscillating fans and delivering them to the neediest families in Little Asia. The moving force in all this was Ron Cowart. He organized and led the Explorer Scouts; he persuaded companies and organizations such as Southwestern Bell Telephone and the Dallas Vietnam Veterans to contribute money and supplies.

Under Ron's supervision, the Explorers gave hundreds of hours of crime prevention instruction in three languages at countless refugee community meetings. In 1987 Explorer Post 68 was selected as Post of the Year in its area because of its community service.

While the Little Asia Explorer troop was developing, other things were happening. The Dallas Police Department decided that it should have an officer who would be a full-time liaison between the department and the Asian community of East Dallas. The decision was that Ron Cowart should be that officer. Ron was pleased, but he knew that if the police were really going to make a difference in the refugee community, there had to be something more than an officer who would work out of central headquarters.

He wanted to see a police officer working right out of the heart of Little Asia, working out of a station that was there to help people in many ways, not only fighting crime but also providing emergency food, clothes for the destitute, transportation to clinics and hospitals, citizenship classes, and other services that would overcome fear and win the confidence of the people. This very special station would be on a busy street, easy to reach, open to everyone. Ron, as he thought about it, called it a "storefront."

No one at police headquarters quarreled with Ron's idea, but, he was told, no money was in the budget to open any kind of station in Little Asia. If he could find the money, the department would give its approval for this unusual kind of venture. So Ron went to the Meadows Foundation, a philanthropic organization, and explained his storefront idea. Foundations like Meadows receive thousands of requests for money every year and must turn down most of them, no matter how worthy. But once more Ron was persuasive. He told them how much money he figured he would need to get started, and he came away with a check for $44,406. He was in business.

The first thing Ron did was recruit three Southeast Asians—Thao Dam, Vietnamese; Leck Keovilay, Laotian; and Pov Thai, Cambodian—who were given training as public service officers. Now there were men in police uniform who could speak the languages and knew the customs of the people of Little Asia.

As soon as he could, Ron installed a five-language "crime-stoppers" hotline at the storefront station. He wanted people to report crimes or the possibility of crimes, but he knew that they wouldn't unless they could report them in their own language. As a result of the hotline, the police have recovered a number of stolen vehicles plus other stolen property; they have made many arrests of criminals because of information provided by the people of Little Asia who once feared the police.

OUR FIRST visit with Ron Cowart was at the storefront. Officially, the storefront's name is the East Dallas Community Police and Refugee Affairs Center, and technically it is a police station. But everyone calls it the storefront, and it is as unlike a police station as anyone could imagine. Once a warehouse, the big room now holds Cowart's desk and desks belonging to the three public service officers. Two other desks are used by volunteers who come in daily to help keep things moving.

Ron was at his desk, a big man, soft-spoken, even-tempered, good-humored. On the wall behind him was an array of photographs of children, adults, family groups, all people who lived or had lived in Little Asia, each photograph with a poignant story attached to it. But every time Ron started to tell us one of the stories, his phone would ring.

"Cowart, storefront," he would say in answer to every call. Then he would listen, making notes on a pad of paper. Someone reported a stolen bicycle; someone was going to take a citizenship test and wanted help with the answers; someone asked for help in finding a job; someone wanted his neighbor arrested for threatening him with a knife. Ron listened and told each person what to do or where to go for the help needed.

The storefront was a beehive of sound and activity. The phones never stopped ringing. People of all ages and nationalities but mostly Asian, poured in and out. Paul said, "I feel like I'm watching a TV sitcom."

A man came in to reclaim a television set that had been stolen from his apartment and recovered by the police. Several women came in for rations of rice. Volunteers were bringing in blankets and other material they had collected from donors. Everything was carried into a back storeroom. Last year alone, Ron told us, the storefront distributed seventy tons of rice, seven hundred oscillating fans, fifteen hundred blankets.

Some of the volunteers bringing in blankets were boys dressed in the uniform of Explorer Post 68, and we asked Ron about them. "They are shy, uncorrupted kids who have blind faith in you," he said. "From the beginning, I insisted on close haircuts, clean fingernails, good personal hygiene, and a big effort in school. There hasn't been a school dropout. Some have graduated from high school now, and some want to become police officers. I still get letters from ones who have moved away.

"I told them from the beginning that I wanted them to become community leaders and get involved in community projects like cleaning up vacant lots and getting people to mark their property so it can be returned if it's stolen and we find it. All this helps demonstrate that police can be compassionate. I tell them that they have to take a person's pain and do something constructive about it and not just laugh at it."

Ron told us that citizenship classes are held at the storefront. At one point sixty-five Vietnamese, Cambodians, and Laotians became citizens at the same time. Since then several hundred more have taken part in the storefront classes.

After a while we went out on the street with Ron and Leck Keovilay, the Lao public service officer. We walked down the hall of an apartment building near the storefront. Ron pointed with satisfaction to the freshly painted walls. One of the many useful things Ron has done is bring pressure on slum landlords. They have paid more than a million dollars in fines, and as a result conditions are improving.

Ron called our attention to the peepholes in all the apartment doors, one of the first community projects of Explorer Post 68. "They give people extra safety," he said. "They can see who is knocking on their door or making trouble in the hall."

We dropped in on an elderly Cambodian woman, whom Ron politely addressed as "grandmother." She lives alone but today was baby-sitting a child who was sick. Her apartment was sparsely furnished; we sat on a mat on the floor.

"She is a very traditional Cambodian," Ron said. "Almost all the older people we have here—and many of the younger ones—suffer from what the psychologists call posttraumatic distress disorder because of the horrible things they witnessed in their countries. She lost her whole family to the Khmer Rouge. They have been violently uprooted from quiet village life and thrust into a way of life they couldn't even imagine. They are lonely, frightened, and frustrated. They don't want to die and be buried in a strange new country. This stress comes out in bodily aches and pains, wife-beating, assault, prostitution, alcoholism.

"For a long time this woman wasn't on welfare because there weren't any translators who could go down and help her apply. At first Southeast Asian children couldn't sign up for free lunch programs because there

Little Asia children are not afraid of this policeman.

were no applications in Cambodian or Lao. The kids went hungry. It was a colossal misunderstanding brought about by an inability to communicate, but the kids were the ones who suffered. Now it's a model program."

Ron didn't say it, but we knew the program became model only after he took large numbers of parents to school board meetings and, with the help of interpreters, was able to make officials understand their problems.

On the way back to the storefront we passed a vacant lot surrounded by a high fence. Once the lot had been a haven for derelicts, drug addicts, and drunks. Ron had helped convert it into a community garden. Seventy-five Asian families had divided it into small plots and each had their own garden just as they had always had in the countries they came from.

Back at the storefront a meeting of Explorer Post 68 was just beginning; they have their meetings in the storeroom behind the main station room. They lined up and recited the Pledge of Allegiance. Most were wearing uniforms, but a few weren't; they had to do push-ups as punishment. The serious business of the day was learning to perform the Heimlich maneuver, a way to force food out of the windpipe in case someone is choking. Ron coached the Explorers and made them practice. Then they planned their Christmas party and decided to go roller skating as part of the festivities.

In a rare quiet moment just before we left the storefront, Paul asked Ron how much longer he thought he would stay with the work in Little Asia. Ron did not answer the question directly, but his meaning was clear when he said, "If I leave, I'll always be wondering what happened to that boy or that girl or that family. They're in my blood now."

He was silent for a moment, then he said, "The more I've been with these people, the more the old wounds have healed. These people have been through hell because there is no pain like the pain of losing your country. Maybe it sounds corny, but they have made me more patriotic about America. I've got a better idea of what it would be like if I lost it."

WE DID not meet Ron's wife, Melinda, during our visit, but later I talked with her on the phone. Like Ron, she is a person who has made a difference. Although she has a doctor's degree in bilingual education, she continues to teach English as a Second Language to Asian students at Spence Middle School, turning down better-paying administrative jobs that would take her away from East Dallas.

"Maybe, someday," she said. "Right now I don't want to disturb what we're doing."

I asked Melinda the question Paul had asked Ron. How much longer would Ron keep at the storefront work?

"I told all our friends I thought he would burn out in a year," Melinda said. "That was three years ago.

"When Ronnie joined the department, what he really wanted to be was a police investigator. He has been offered a promotion to investigator four times since he started at the storefront. He has turned it down four times. I guess that's the answer to your question."

"Yes," I said, "I guess it is."

The Big House with
a Big Heart

CAROLE POPE is a quiet-talking woman who seems to be holding back enormous, impatient energy. Her office reflects her total commitment to her work. Shelves of law books stand beside a tank of fish. The walls are filled with framed letters from correction authorities, judges, and city council members, all praising her work. A few pictures of babies hang beside the letters. On the back of the door is a poster picture of a sunset bearing the words, "Tomorrow Is a New Beginning."

The phone never stopped ringing the morning we met her. After one call Carole laughed and said, "I go from the sublime to the ridiculous in this work. That was a judge who wants me to coach her daughter in singing tonight so she can perform tomorrow. I taught music before I went to prison. I'll coach her, and the next time I need help for one of my clients, I'll remind her of the favor. This place is really something, the most unorthodox place in the world."

"This place" is a huge old Victorian house located on Hoyt Avenue in a pleasant middle-class neighborhood in northwest Portland, Oregon. Built in 1911, its forty-four rooms qualified it as a mansion at that time.

Today it is furnished with secondhand or donated chairs, couches, and other furniture which doesn't always match and can be a bit shabby. But everything is clean and comfortable, and the feeling is homey. A few rugs are scattered about; the window curtains are simple but cheerful. The upstairs living room has a large television set, and a visitor must be careful not to step on toys lying on the floor.

The house is technically a prison for most of the fifteen to twenty-five women who live there at any one time as part of a program called Our New Beginnings, but for many it is the only decent home they have ever had. Some have been assigned to the program by judges as an alternative to their being sent to the penitentiary; some have been placed here as part of a prison early-release program; a few are "self-referrals," who know they need the support that Our New Beginnings can give. All are offenders or ex-offenders who have run afoul of the law because of drug addiction, prostitution, theft, and other violations of the law.

"We try to make them feel that this is their home," Carole said, looking at pictures on the wall of some of the thirty-nine babies born during the past year to women who lived in the house.

Carole Pope is the originator and director of Our New Beginnings, a program born out of a life that gives her complete understanding of the women who come to the house. "My childhood had a lot of ups and downs," she told us. "My parents were alcoholics. It was a dysfunctional family. My father committed suicide, and my mother died of alcoholism. They loved me, but they were damaged people who didn't know how to raise a child.

"I'm a recovering alcoholic. I started drinking early to escape the reality of my home. The last six years and four I spent in the penitentiary are the only dry periods of my life. For a while, before prison, I had a life going. I got a master's degree in music and taught music in college. I did a lot of good things, but I was too damaged. I sometimes wonder what I could have done if I had been sober. When I made my mistake I was drinking an immense amount."

Her mistake was to forge papers in order to steal silver. She was convicted of forgery and first-degree theft and sentenced to two five-year terms in the Oregon Women's Correctional Center. She has vivid, nightmarish memories of being taken to the prison, the stripsearch by prison matrons, putting on the prison uniform, entering her cell for the first time and hearing the door click shut behind her. She remembers the anger and the stark fear.

"I was in prison twenty-one months, and then I was paroled. Getting out of prison is terrifying. It's like standing outside and looking in through a window. They expect you to come back rehabilitated, humble, contrite. Instead, you reappear with no more skills than you went in with, no money, no place to stay. Most women end up some place where drugs, alcohol, and prostitution are everywhere around them.

"The first time out, there was nobody for me to talk to. My parole officer was a man, and I was the only woman in his case load. We were at each other's throats all the time. He said I was rebelling against authority, and he sent me back to prison.

"My first night back was the best night's sleep I had had in four months. It may sound crazy, but compared to life outside, prison is easy. You're scared at first, but you get into a routine. They run your life for you."

But it was not really a life inside those walls, Carole knew, not for her, not for all the other women that she saw come in, go out, and all too tragically often come back again. "Some women left on parole and ended up back in the joint within twenty-four hours," Carole said. "There wasn't any real effort to get them ready to go out, to rehabilitate them. They were just kept penned up until it was time to release them."

The next time Carole Pope was offered parole she turned it down because she had made up her mind that she was going to do something to help herself and to help as many other women like her as she could. A new Oregon law specified that every prison had to have a law library and a trained inmate paralegal who could help other inmates with legal matters. With her educational background, Carole decided that she could become a paralegal and she did, the first paralegal at the women's correctional center to be trained by the Oregon attorney general's office. She put a law library together in the prison and began to help other inmates with legal problems.

At the same time, Carole began to talk to other inmates about what could be done to help women on parole cut down the odds of being recommitted. "There were nine of us," Carole recalled. "We formed a support group and discussed ways to keep ourselves and others like us from going back to jail once we were free. We would talk about how to get jobs, how to find a friend who would talk sense to us, how to get money, clothes, even the most commonplace things like toothpaste. We talked for a year, put our ideas together, and dreamed up Our New Beginnings. We actually incorporated it while I was still in prison, in 1981."

After twenty-eight months Carole was given parole again, in November, 1981. "I emerged from prison with nothing except two pair of jeans, two shirts, and tennis shoes in a little plastic bag. That's all." This time, however, she had an understanding parole officer. "She literally saved my life," Carole said. "She became a strong support with whom I talked every day."

With her paralegal training, Carole was able to get a job working for a Portland attorney. Now she had a place in society; now she had money for an apartment, clothes, a car. That might have been the end of the prison dream of Our New Beginnings; none of the other eight women who helped develop the idea in prison stuck with it. But Carole couldn't get it out of her mind. She couldn't forget the scores of women she had known at the Oregon Women's Correctional Center who were going to need special help to stay out of prison once they were out on parole.

Carole made up her mind that she would make Our New Beginnings work. "I'm stubborn," she said, "and I was obsessed with the idea of making it work. I still am."

In her vision, Our New Beginnings would be a place where a woman on parole could have a decent home while she worked her way back into society. It would be a place where she would be helped to get job training, health care, drug counseling, training in being a good parent, and other assistance that she might need. Carole even hoped that judges might send some women offenders to live at Our New Beginnings instead of sending them to prison.

"But I had no idea what to do," Carole said. "I didn't know how to talk to people. I had no money, and I didn't know anything about requesting grants from foundations or the city or county governments."

She made herself start talking to people. Every hour that she wasn't working at her law office job she talked to judges, to the county attorney's staff, to other county and city judicial and law enforcement officials, anyone who would take the time to listen to her ideas about a new way to treat women in trouble with the law.

"It took me a year to convince the local legal system that what I wanted to do wasn't a scam," she said.

Finally, one judge took a chance and sent a woman parolee to Our New Beginnings for counseling. Carole got a small grant from Multnomah County and another from the city of Portland. She was assigned another client and then another.

"I knew we had to have a house," Carole said, "so we rented this one. It was right for us, big, in a good, quiet neighborhood. We had no money for rent. The real estate agent who found the house for us donated her commission, which paid the rent for the first two months. Our finances were like a big patchwork quilt, but somehow we made it. I was still working as a paralegal and using my salary to meet expenses. Ten days before the rent was due, we got a grant from the Fred Meyer Trust. The check was for $47,000. I couldn't believe it. I cried for days. I just looked and looked at that check. I still have a photocopy of it. We kept going from there. Our money problems are never over, but we've been at it for seven years now."

During those years more than fifteen hundred women have been assigned to Our New Beginnings by judges and parole boards. Hundreds have lived in the big house on Hoyt Street for varying lengths of time; others have taken part in the program as nonresidents. Carole Pope's case load averages about fifty women at any one time, fifteen to twenty living

Carole Pope with Our New Beginnings residents.

in the house, the others living outside but reporting in regularly to take part in Our New Beginnings activities.

Every woman is helped in finding a job if she needs one. Our New Beginnings has developed strong ties to agencies and industries that sponsor on-the-job training. Seventy percent of the women in Our New Beginnings have at least one child. These women take part in weekly maternal education meetings and are visited by home health nurses. Pregnant women who have been drug addicts are carefully monitored and given special attention. Baby clothes, toys, baby furniture, and other necessities are donated to Our New Beginnings and given to the women with infants.

To fight drug addiction, experienced and certified drug counselors are brought in; every woman in the Our New Beginnings program must attend a drug meeting once a week, those with a history of drug use, twice a week. Individual drug counseling is also available. A weekly group discusses AIDS and AIDS prevention.

Women who are sent to Our New Beginnings as an alternative to prison are often in poor health because of drug or alcohol use, poor nutrition, no decent medical attention, and emotional stress. At Our New Beginnings they get a healthy diet; needed medical treatment is arranged; they get the rest they need through structured sleep hours.

Job training and placement, health care, child care, and parental education are major elements of Our New Beginnings, but the program goes far beyond those essentials. Transportation to and from work is arranged, literacy tutoring is given, as is anger- and stress-reduction counseling. Group recreational activities are set up: beach and zoo trips, carnival outings, pizza parties, and more.

"I work with from two to three hundred women every year," Carole said. "The money I spend doing this wouldn't keep more than twelve women in prison. There is a crisis of overcrowding in the prison system. Right now there are 142 women inmates in a correctional center built for 72. I get a majority of those coming out on the street. It is a corrupt system that sends women out with no skills, no money, into an environment where drugs and prostitution are everywhere."

90

Carole Pope has a large amount of anger just below the surface, and it shows when she is talking about the "system" and the women who come to Our New Beginnings. "Most of them are hardcore addicts," she said, "women who have been on drugs ten years or more." And she added a terrible statistic: "Ninety percent or more of our clients were victims of child abuse. They need all the help they can get."

Perhaps the greatest help they receive comes from Carole herself. She is available to them around the clock, day and night, seven days a week. She will talk and listen, show them affection when they need it, be tough on them when toughness is called for. She has tracked down runaways in the middle of the night and brought them back to the house. One of the women died in her arms from an overdose of drugs.

The women in the program find out soon enough what kind of person Carole Pope is. "If you want to help yourself, there are no holds barred," said one resident at Our New Beginnings house. "She will help you. If not, she will send you back to jail."

A resident called Red was paroled and sent to Our New Beginnings. "At first I didn't want to come," she said. "I was just going to stay in jail. I heard all these rumors, like they locked you up in a cage. But that's not true. Now it feels like this is my family."

Another resident talked about the rigid routines: a woman in the program has to get permission even to go out for an errand and certainly for a rare weekend away; she can use the telephone only at certain times and has to take her turn for a shower. But she also talked about the good things, the comfort and support, and just the simple pleasure of waking up in the morning to the smell of homemade cinnamon rolls.

Other comments about Carole Pope from women in the program run in the same vein:

"She's a beautiful person to me. She has turned my life around."

"She will go to bat for you, go through the fire, but put you back in jail at a heartbeat if you prove to her that's where you deserve to be."

"She's tough."

"If she wasn't, we would walk all over her."

"I have lots of patience because I know these women so well," Carole said. "I know they'll make mistakes. All I ask of them is that they don't lie to me. They live with lifetime habits. They don't know how to deal with people who hug them and don't expect anything in return. These women are throwaways. I get real angry at the system and fight it all the time, even though I have to work within it."

The system—law enforcement, legal, judicial—has finally realized that Carole Pope and Our New Beginnings are making a difference, a big difference, for these throwaway women. The success rate of her program—success in the sense that the women who take part in it have not become law offenders again—is an impressive 64 percent. Successful participation in the program may last from a few weeks to several months, depending upon the nature of the problems to be overcome such as learning a job skill, finding a job, overcoming a drug problem.

Multnomah Court Justice R. E. Jones of Portland calls Carole one of the most credible people in the criminal justice system. "I have complete faith in her and her judgment," he said.

For her part Carole wishes the system would acknowledge her work with better financial support. "This year's budget is $268,000," she said. "It should be $350,000. We're always close to bankruptcy. But I won't give up until all of my gals have jobs and a place back in society."

Carole Pope knows that she will be at her work for a long time.

Max

THIS IS a story that Damon Runyon would have loved, that gifted creator of tough guys with hearts of gold in *Guys and Dolls* and *Little Miss Marker,* the creator of Nicely-Nicely Jones, Horse Thief, Willie the Worrier, and so many other colorful "characters" from Boston and "citizens" from New York.

Max Silk is not a character from Boston or a citizen from New York. Detroit is his town and has been for more than fifty years. Max owns and runs the Left Field Deli in the very shadow of the Detroit Tigers baseball stadium; for more than twenty years loyal customers have come from all over the city and beyond to sit at the Left Field's yellow Formica counter and eat hot pastrami sandwiches, corned beef and cabbage, Boston clam chowder (Fridays only), and Max's special corn bread (everyday).

Max is Jewish, and items on his deli menu reflect that fact: chopped liver, gefilte fish, lox and cream cheese, kosher franks. But Max's customers span every religion and race, every economic class from hard-hat, blue-collar worker to the gray pin-striped-suited lawyer who brings an out-of-town client to try some of Max's short ribs of beef.

On my first visit to the Left Field Deli, lunch was in full swing, and it took me a while to capture a stool at the counter. I shook hands briefly with Max, whom I had talked with on the phone, and then he was moving down the counter, carrying food, saying hello to a regular, sometimes stopping for what seemed like a serious conversation. Once I heard him talking to someone about a boys' camp.

The man on my right looked like a Left Field regular, and I asked, "What's the best thing on the menu?"

"What I'm eating," he said. "Potato pancakes, sour cream, and applesauce. They just make them on Wednesdays."

So I had potato pancakes, and if there was anything better on the menu, I wouldn't have wanted to know about it. My menu guide's name was Seamus O'Brien; he owned a warehouse across the street and ate most of his lunches at the Left Field. I told Seamus I hoped to put Max in a book.

"You can't imagine how many friends he has," Seamus said. "I hope you'll be kind to him in your book."

Max had come out from behind the counter and was talking intently to a newly arrived woman dressed in a smart business suit. "Max seems to do lots of business besides serving food," I said.

"Lots of business," Seamus said. "All of it good."

After the last customer had eaten the last piece of cheese cake, Max Silk and I had a chance to talk. Detroit was indeed his town, Max assured me, but he hadn't been born here. His parents immigrated from Germany to Canton, Ohio, in 1906, and Max had been born there in 1907. Soon the family moved to Cleveland, and that was where Max had spent most of his boyhood.

Apparently, it was far from a tranquil boyhood. "I was expelled from every school in Cleveland," Max said.

No doubt Max was exaggerating, but he left no doubt that his had been a rough, tough young manhood. In 1924 his family moved to Detroit, and Max's way of life on the edge did not change. He spoke vaguely of bringing things across the border from Canada. In time he

Max Silk

became a bookie, taking bets on horse races, football and baseball games, and other sporting events.

Max's territory was Detroit's skid row. One day when he was out collecting his bets, Max saw a Catholic priest handing out coins to some of the down-and-out men slouched against the buildings and sitting in doorways. Max thought nothing of this at the time, but two weeks later—on a Monday after he had done very well on weekend football bets—he saw the priest again passing out coins.

To this day Max cannot tell you exactly what impulse moved him; it was not something that was a part of his nature. But when he passed the priest, Max stopped, dug two twenty-dollar bills out of his pocket, and handed them to the astonished clergyman. Then Max walked on.

He had no way to know it, of course, but in that single moment, that single act of generosity, Max Silk turned his life around. The man he gave the twenty-dollar bills to was the Right Reverend Clement Kern, a priest whose life was dedicated to uplifting the downtrodden, to fighting for better housing for inner city families, jobs for the jobless, shelter for the homeless, better education for children of the slums. This priest became known as the "Legend of Porter Street"—where his church was located—because of his dedication to the poor and his ability to get things done for them. When Father Kern was killed in a tragic car accident in 1983, a statue to him was erected near Kerns Gardens, a housing development that he had worked to build.

Father Kern did not know Max Silk, but he knew there was something behind Max's gift that should be encouraged. He found out who Max was and went to see him. At that moment began a friendship that lasted almost four decades. Slowly Father Kern drew Max into charitable work such as helping to start a new soup kitchen, a shelter for the homeless, a clothing drive for inner city children. If Max resisted the gentle pressure from the priest, he does not remember it today. He does remember that Father Kern was very persuasive.

During this time—again with the encouragement of Father Kern—Max made the decision to get out of shady bookie work and go into the food business. He tried a pizza place, a barbecue place, other things, but nothing quite worked until he opened the Left Field Deli in 1968. Getting it off the ground was not easy, but the deli worked. Max recalls that Father Kern loved the Left Field. He never missed clam chowder on Friday if he could help it, and he usually brought along some businessman or community leader whose help he wanted in starting a new project for the disadvantaged.

"He just liked to be here," Max told me, speaking of Father Kern. "Sometimes he would get behind the counter and pour coffee or help clean up if we were too busy."

The Temple-Trumbull area north of Tiger Stadium is one of the poorest in Detroit. More than 52 percent of this racially and ethnically mixed neighborhood live below the federal poverty level. It was only natural that Max Silk should become a charter member and chief promoter of a neighborhood organization called FOCUS, Inc. (Friends Offering Challenge, Understanding, and Service) that was set up in the seventies to improve the quality of life in this area. It was only natural, too, that the Left Field Deli became an unofficial but very active meeting place for much of the development work that went on.

Sister Helen Huellmantel, whose order is Sisters of St. Joseph, was a prime mover of FOCUS, Inc., in its formative years. "The Left Field Deli was my second office," she told me. "We would invite a group of important people who could help us in our work. The group would always start with breakfast at Max's or end with lunch there. These breakfasts and lunches were always at Max's expense, and they gave him a chance to talk to everyone."

Max put his own money into FOCUS, Inc., and he was not shy—and still is not—about talking his regular customers into making contributions to FOCUS, Inc., activities and other programs that he feels strongly about.

"When he is talking to you," Sister Helen said, "Max makes you feel you are the only person in the world who can help him with the particular problem he is working on." Then, referring to Father Clement Kern, Sister Helen added, "Of course, Max learned from the master."

Three of FOCUS, Inc.'s, most successful on-going activities are a

Max Silk's support helped this neighborhood center become a success.

The Sunshine Montessori School which Max Silk supported from the beginning.

youth center for boys and girls, ages 7 to 17, the Sunshine Montessori School for children ages 2½ to 6, and a neighborhood center for adults. Max Silk was a supporter of everyone of these neighborhood successes and still is.

Max spends a great deal of time running the deli and a great deal of time promoting FOCUS, Inc., and other charitable activities. But he makes time to keep in personal touch with the neighborhood by bringing from ten to fifteen boys and girls in once a week for breakfast at the Left Field.

"We talk and they call me Uncle Max," he told me, a look of great satisfaction on his face. "I get my rewards."

Max attends a synagogue downtown and takes his religion seriously, although he has spent much of his life supporting neighborhood charities promoted by the Catholic Church. "It is here that they need my help," Max said.

In 1987 Max's customers got together and contributed three thousand dollars to give him a surprise birthday trip to Israel. Max simply beamed when he told me about this, but he said, "They just wanted to get rid of me for a while."

Max's smile, however, said that he knew how much love had been behind that birthday surprise.

Hope

BY SOME estimates three million people in the United States today are homeless, over half a million of them children. That figure is greater than the population of Iowa. These men, women, children, and babies in their parents' arms wander the streets of every American city looking for a place to sleep, a night's shelter, a hot meal. In just one city, Los Angeles, twenty-five-thousand homeless walk the streets every day. Nearly one-third of them suffer from chronic mental illness.

America's failure to provide even minimum protection for these most vulnerable victims of social breakdown has been called the shame of a great nation.

BROTHER Ronald Giannoni knows about homelessness, about hunger, about hopelessness. He knows that these social evils are not confined to the dreary inner cities of Los Angeles, New York, Philadelphia, Washington, D.C. They are all around him in the pleasant little city of Wilmington, Delaware, population seventy thousand, where he has lived and worked for the last eleven years. During those years, he has been the moving, driving spirit behind a community effort that has opened three Emmanuel Dining Rooms to feed the hungry, three Mary Mother of Hope Houses to shelter homeless and destitute women, a House of Joseph for homeless men, and a job placement center to help both men and women gain a foothold back in society.

A short man with intense youthful energy, Brother Ronald wears sandals and the chocolate-brown robe of his order of Capuchin friars. When you first meet Brother Ronald, you think for a moment—but only a moment—of the tranquility of a medieval monastery. The robe brings up that image, of course, but perhaps there is something else, a look in Brother Ronald's eyes that tells you he knows exactly who he is and why he has chosen to do the kind of work he does in this world.

But then you hear the flat Bronx accent of his native New York, and you are no longer in an Italian monastery garden. You are, as Paul and I were that morning, in Brother Ronald's small office in Wilmington. The office is in an old building—once a political club, Brother Ronald thinks—almost under a railroad bridge in a rundown part of the city. This is headquarters of the Ministry of Caring, the organization that Brother Ronald has built, food kitchen by food kitchen, shelter by shelter, over the course of a decade.

Brother Ronald's head is full of figures, and they come out in a rush. "Last year we provided 134,882 meals to needy people who would have gone hungry if the Emmanuel Dining Rooms hadn't been there," he said. "Two thousand women have been sheltered at the first Mary Mother of Hope House we opened in 1977. But last year alone we had to refuse 1,406 requests for emergency shelter at Hope House II because every room was full. For every family we accept we have to say no to six families."

Brother Ronald looked at the ceiling, as if seeking just the right words. "It's incredible," he said, "that a small city of seventy thousand can have such a problem with homelessness. It's very sad. Is America becoming like Calcutta?"

He stopped and thought a moment before continuing. "The two big problems are affordable housing and mental illness. Rents are going up all the time. Poor families can't pay those rents. They get thrown out on the street. People break down. There are people walking the streets who would have been institutionalized a few years ago. They are people caught in a crisis, a lost job, a lost house, maybe a drug crisis, bankruptcy. These people don't know anything about how to live on the street, but that's what they're doing."

Without any more talk, Brother Ronald drove us to one of the houses that shelters families. "Come see for yourself," he said.

The family shelter is a row house, and half a dozen family groups were sitting in the big living room-dining room common area when we arrived. The first woman we talked to had a small girl sitting on each side of her and held a baby boy, perhaps a year old, on her lap. "We're here because my house caught on fire, and we lost everything," the woman told us. "We were suddenly out on the street, just walking. Here we have a roof, good food, a place to keep clean. I don't know what we would do if we couldn't stay here."

A thin young woman was feeding applesauce to her baby. "I got hurt on my job," she said, "and got disability payments. Then the payments stopped. The landlord put a padlock on my door when I got behind on the rent."

Another woman with a six-month-old baby had a similar story. "My rent was too high, and they moved me out on the street when I got behind. Landlords don't have a heart. The lowest rent I could find was four hundred dollars a month, plus a security deposit. There was no way I could afford that."

We met a woman who was working as a bus driver for the city. She had lost her apartment for violating a public housing code against over-crowding. "I've got five kids," she said. "We were thrown out of our apartment because we didn't have enough bedrooms. I need three bed-rooms, but I can't afford a place that big."

FROM THE time he was a fifth-grade student in the Bronx, Brother Ronald knew that he wanted to become a Capuchin friar. One day a

Brother Ronald at a shelter for homeless families.

member of this Franciscan order visited Ronald's school and talked about how the Capuchins worked with the poor people of Africa. He explained the mission of the Capuchins to help the poorest of the poor, those in greatest need, wherever they may be in the world. He said that the goal of the Capuchins was to follow the Gospel of Christ according to St. Francis of Assisi.

"I never changed my mind after that," Brother Ronald said. "I knew what I wanted to be, and I knew what I wanted to do."

Another powerful influence in his life moved him in the same direction. Ronald was one of seven children and was only three years old when his father died in 1953. Ronald grew up watching his mother work as a seamstress from morning until night six days a week to feed and clothe her family.

"But she was never so poor or so tired that she couldn't help other people in our neighborhood whose need was greater than ours," Brother Ronald said. "And she always taught us that if God closes a door, He opens a window. And there is always hope in an open window."

Brother Ronald entered the Capuchin community in 1969 in Beacon, New York, and professed his final vows as a Capuchin friar in 1975. He was sent to Wilmington and arrived with a vision of a ministry that would devote itself entirely to the poor of the city. He had a name in mind, The Ministry of Caring.

"How did you know there would be a need?" I asked. "That there would be poor and homeless people in Wilmington?"

And just as I should have known he would, Brother Ronald quoted the Gospel according to Matthew: "For ye have the poor always with you."

What Brother Ronald discovered was shocking: in the entire state of Delaware there was not a single shelter for homeless and destitute women. That discovery led to the creation of the first Mary Mother of Hope House in 1977.

"I wanted to get hope into the name," Brother Ronald said. "I wanted it because of the hope my mother always had and because that's what our work is all about. To find the means of giving hope back to people who have lost hope."

From that beginning has followed all the rest: the other Hope houses, the Emmanuel Dining Rooms, the St. Joseph shelter for men, the job placement center. Brother Ronald gives the highest praise to scores of other churches, synagogues, and civic groups that support the dining rooms and other activities of the Ministry of Caring.

"Wilmington is a little city with a big heart," Brother Ronald said.

I asked Brother Ronald if he thought that, as a nation, we have come to accept a throwaway class of people, a poor homeless class that we just have to learn to live with.

Brother Ronald bristled at that idea. "Absolutely not," he said. "There is more attention to the poor and homeless today than there was even during the Depression. Every newspaper, every television network is concerned. Homelessness and poverty have become the number one issue before the nation. President Bush has pushed it up to the top of his concern."

"In other words, there is hope," I said.

Brother Ronald smiled and said firmly, "There is hope."

4

Making a Difference
by Personal Example

Valerie Pida

"I Won't Let Cancer Dominate My Life"

VALERIE PIDA was twelve, living in Germany with her U.S. Air Force father, mother, brothers, and sister, when the first sign of trouble came— a lump on her neck. "It was just one of those crazy lumps you get when you're twelve years old," Valerie said. "I didn't think much about it."

But her mother took her to a hospital, and they were told it was nothing to worry about, just to put a heating pad on it. More lumps came and spread under her arms, but the hospital verdict was still that it was nothing serious.

When the family returned to the United States and settled in Las Vegas, Nevada, however, the cruel truth was revealed. To play volleyball at her junior high school, Valerie had to have a physical examination. The examining doctor spotted the lumps and recommended an immediate biopsy. The result: Valerie had cancer, a form called Hodgkin's disease that is prone to attack young people. It invades the lymphatic system and bone structure and destroys the body's ability to fight infection. The result is weight loss, fatigue, fever—and sometimes death.

"I looked up Hodgkin's disease in an encyclopedia," Valerie said, "and it said I had a fatal disease. But my doctors told me that was an old encyclopedia. They told me Hodgkin's disease had become treatable."

Yes, it was treatable. Valerie Pida is twenty-one years old now, a junior at the University of Nevada at Las Vegas (UNLV), and her ten-year fight with cancer is a true odyssey of the human spirit. We met Valerie at the UNLV gymnasium one morning when she would normally have been going to cheerleader practice. Paul wanted to get a picture of her in action. But she had suffered a muscle injury the day before and could hardly walk, so we sat under a tree and talked.

As we were settling down, another student came by. He stopped and wanted to talk to Valerie about his cancer treatment; under his shirt we could see a catheter which was feeding medicine into his system. "I've heard about Valerie ever since I came here two years ago," the boy said. "We have the same nurse."

Later, Valerie said, "I like to talk with them. It helps. I've talked to lots of young people with cancer. They're confused, afraid. I don't try to tell them it won't be hard and painful, but they can look at me and see I'm still here."

The battle began in junior high school. Valerie had her initial surgery in 1981 and started chemotherapy and radiation treatment. Chemotherapy is a combination of powerful drugs which attack multiplying cancer cells; the combination differs from person to person. Many formulas may be tried, sometimes to no avail. Radiation, or radiotherapy, tries to destroy cancer cells with invisible beams of energy called X rays or gamma rays.

From the very beginning Valerie made up her mind that she was not going to be just a cancer victim on whom everyone took pity. "I was going to be a teenager and a student and have cancer, too, if that had to be," she told us.

In junior high Valerie tried out for cheerleader and made the squad. She played volleyball and made straight *A*'s in her school subjects.

"I handled cancer like it was another activity," Valerie said. "I just fitted it into my schedule like cheerleader practice and math. Sometimes I'd have chemotherapy after school, be sick all night, and then go back to school the next day. Sometimes I'd sit in the bathroom at school and be sick and study at the same time so I wouldn't have to miss an exam."

Valerie talks matter-of-factly, easily, almost cheerfully about years of the most harrowing treatments. Her conversation is filled with references to catheters, full-body radiation, lead cobalt, five hundred rads, ABVD (a course of drug treatment which gets it name from the drugs involved), MOPP, a different course of drugs, VP-16, still another drug.

"VP-16 causes amnesia," Valerie said. "I went bananas with it, and it took three nurses to get me back in bed.

"Of course, you lose your hair. I've been bald three times."

And then she said, "It's odd, I know. I've never looked at it, the cancer, in a negative way. It's just a part of my life. I worry more about my parents than I do myself because they have always been so frightened, and they've had to work so hard because of the expense."

Valerie talked about her hair again. "It always comes back. That makes me happy."

The fight against the deadly enemy continued through high school. Valerie went out for cheerleader and again made the squad. Twice the cancer went into remission, when she was sixteen and eighteen, but each time it forced its way back into her system.

After graduating from high school, Valerie enrolled at UNLV and once again went out for and made the cheerleader squad. Was there some psychological reason she wanted to be a cheerleader? I asked. Did it fill some deep-down need?

"I just like to cheer," Valerie said.

It was after Valerie had settled into her college program that her doctors brought up the possibility of a bone marrow transplant. There was no other chance for her to survive, they concluded. The chemotherapy, the radiation were no longer working effectively enough to keep her alive. But, the doctors warned, the chances of her surviving the transplant were no more than 30 percent at the most.

"I told the doctors, let's do it," Valerie said. "Let's don't even talk about it. I got the bone marrow from my brother John. I was very lucky because he was a perfect match. I know somebody who has seven brothers and sisters, and none of them matched."

Before the transplant could take place, money had to be raised to pay for it and for the years of treatment and monitoring that would follow, if Valerie survived the initial operation. Las Vegas civic clubs, newspapers, television, and radio mounted a campaign to raise the $125,000 that would be needed. The response was generous; money also came in from all over the country because Valerie had been seen cheerleading at UNLV Runnin' Rebels basketball games on national television, and the story of her desperate need had become known. The full amount needed was quickly raised and placed in a trust fund for the operation, which would take place at the City of Hope Hospital, a famous cancer research and treatment facility in Duarte, California.

"Again I was lucky," Valerie said. "It was the best place to go, and I was fortunate to be accepted. There are so many sick people who never have a chance for this special treatment."

John Pida, Valerie's brother, flew in from his U.S. Air Force assignment in Germany, and the bone marrow transplant took place on April 21, 1987. The delicate, four-hour operation involved the transfusion of three-fourths of a quart of John's healthy bone marrow into Valerie's veins. Then began the tense, frightening weeks in a high-isolation room that would determine whether her body would accept her brother's bone marrow or reject it and whether the new marrow would resist the cancer. Her doctors called the first three months after the transplant critical; if she lived two years beyond that, they said, her chances of leading a normal, healthy life were 95 percent.

The battle was joined in isolation: more chemotherapy and radiation to fight the cancer while the new bone marrow took hold, antibiotics to stave off viral infections; she ate special antibacterial food; she saw nothing but hospital gowns and face masks.

"I was sick," Valerie said, "just sick." She recalled a particularly low moment in isolation. "I was hooked up to four different IV pumps at the same time."

But after three months Valerie left the City of Hope and flew back to

Las Vegas to be with her family and to reenter the university. She was bald again, and she had to wear an antibacterial mask when she went around the campus. But she was back.

"The doctors wanted me to take a year off after the transplant," Valerie said, "but I told them there was no way I could do that. I wanted to get back to my studies, get back to cheering. I told them I'd compromise. I'd go part time and see if I could handle it. I remember those first cheering sessions were so hard because I had lost all my muscles."

Does she ever feel sorry for herself? "No way," Valerie said. "I look at myself and say, 'Hey, you're lucky. You can walk, you can cheer. You lead an active, normal life. Don't complain. Look at the people who exist in wheelchairs, in bed, who are paralyzed.' Once in a hospital I met a boy in a wheelchair. The day after he graduated from high school, he was on top of the world, and then he had a surfing accident. He said to me, 'You're the kind of person I like to talk to because you don't quit.'"

Valerie is studying mathematics at UNLV but has begun to think that she might like to switch into the news and media field. "I want to inform people," she said. In addition to her studies, cheerleading, and medical treatments, Valerie works thirty-two hours a week in a video store. "When do I study? My books are always with me. I study whenever I can."

Valerie's story is still being written. Her transplant was about a year-and-a-half behind her when we met her. She returns to the City of Hope Hospital every month for monitoring and treatment; tests are not conclusive yet. But one thing is certain, and it was the last thing Valerie said to us:

"I won't let cancer dominate my life."

Something Special

EVERY YEAR the Boys Clubs of America select a National Youth of the Year. Each of six hundred Boys Clubs (or Boys and Girls Clubs in some cities) throughout the United States nominates a member for this honor. Since the membership of all local clubs totals 1.3 million, the pool of well-qualified candidates is large and the competition for the award is spirited. Of many criteria for the award, scholastic achievement, leadership, community service, and success in overcoming some physical or economic disability are especially important.

In 1987 the Boys Clubs of America chose Kenneth McBride, eighteen years old, as National Youth of the Year. Nominated by the Boys and Girls Club of Salem, Oregon, where he had been a member since the age of eight, Ken McBride had a background worthy of this honor. He was a member of the National Honor Society; his score on a national scholastic aptitude test put him in the top one percent of his age group. He had varsity high school letters in basketball, baseball, and football. He was cocaptain of the basketball team and Athlete of the Year in his senior year. He had served his North Salem High School and the community in many ways: as student representative on the Community School Advisory Committee, as chairman of his class Community Food Basket Drive, as a member of a drug and alcohol awareness program for fifth and sixth graders, as a participant in rest-home visits to the elderly.

On September 23, 1987, in an award ceremony at the White House, President Ronald Reagan installed Ken McBride as Boys Club of America Youth of the Year. For Ken there followed a parade with marching band through the streets of Salem, a Ken McBride Day at North Salem High School, and a spot in the Fiesta Bowl parade with other "superkids" chosen in various competitions. There also followed a year of speech-making and meetings with civic and youth groups and of representing the Boys Clubs of America at both U.S. and international conferences.

Ken delayed college enrollment for a year so that he could give his Youth of the Year activities the attention they deserved. In September, 1988, with those responsibilities behind him, he entered the University of Oregon. A scholarship from *Reader's Digest,* part of the Youth of the Year Award, helped with tuition and living expenses.

I TALKED with Maggie McBride, Ken's mother, before I talked with Ken. I already knew some of the family history, how her marriage had collapsed when Ken was four years old, how Maggie had assumed total care and support of Ken and of Ken's older brother and sister, Cameron, eleven, and Melodi, thirteen.

Maggie McBride is a person who talks easily about herself, her children, and her life experiences. "After the marriage breakup, I took the children to the home of my foster father in California," she said. "That was no solution, but I didn't know what else to do. We had left everything in Oklahoma. Suddenly we had nothing. I had no idea how to make a living. I had no idea what to do. I just sat in the living room and cried.

"One day, after we had been at my foster father's for a while, Ken came into the living room. I was there crying, as usual. Ken was four years old, remember. He stood looking at me and then he said quietly, 'Mama, if you don't stop crying, I'm going to start.' "

President Ronald Reagan installs Ken McBride as Boys Clubs of America National Youth of the Year for 1987. Photograph by Ankers Photographers, Inc.

That woke her up, Maggie said. It made her realize that she had to do something, and it made her realize that Ken was "something special." With a simple statement, he had pushed the button that made her go into action. What she did was take her children to Oregon, where she had spent some of her growing-up years. In Salem, she found a part-time job at Chemeketa Community College and another part-time job at a cannery. She rented a small apartment, and the O'Brien family, mother and three children, settled down for life in Salem. After a few years the older children left, Cameron for the army, Melodi to college—working to pay her way.

"Times were hard," Maggie McBride said. "We moved around Salem house-sitting, living in people's houses and taking care of them while the people were away on long trips. That way we didn't have to pay rent, but it was hard moving so much. That never seemed to bother Ken, though, and he was always encouraging me. He would say, 'You don't have to worry. We'll get along.'

"But he knew how serious our financial problems were. Once when he was seven years old, I asked him to go to the store for some milk and peanut butter and a few other things. I gave him a five-dollar bill. *The* five-dollar bill. It was near the end of the month, and that was all the money we had left until payday. He was gone a long time, and when he came back he had no groceries, and his face was chalk-white. 'I lost it,' he said. 'I lost the five dollars.' It had slipped through a hole in his pocket.

"Ken would not go to bed. After a while he just took off, and again he was gone a long time. But I will never forget the look on his face when he came back. I have never seen such a happy face. 'I found it,' he said, and he handed me the five-dollar bill."

I asked Maggie if she could single out one characteristic of Ken's that had helped him excel.

"Determination," she said. "When he decides to do something, he doesn't know how to quit until he has done it."

"Can you give me an example?" I asked.

"I can give you a hundred," Maggie said, "but here is one. When Ken was a junior, he made the high school baseball team, but he hardly ever got to play because his batting was not good enough. The whole season he just sat on the bench and played only if someone got hurt. All the next fall and winter he worked on his swing. He got a videotape on batting, and he almost wore it out studying, practicing. In his senior year he made the team again. He played every game. He batted over .400 and was named Athlete of the Year."

I asked Maggie how Ken got started in the Boys Club. "I took him there when he was about eight," she said. "I knew he needed more help than I could give him. And he got it at the Boys Club, help in sports and studying and in ideas about community service. He found the role models I hoped he would find. I was working at two jobs then, and I was sometimes late picking him up at night. I would drive up to the Boys Club on cold, dark evenings in my old Ford Pinto, and two people would be standing on the front steps—Ken and a staff member—waiting for me. As he got older, Ken became a volunteer and a leader in the club."

"Now that Ken is in college, how are you going to spend your extra time?" I asked Maggie.

"We're both in college," Maggie said. "I've been working on my bachelor's degree in English a little bit at a time for years. Now, I'm going to finish it."

The first time I talked to Ken, he was home from the university for a weekend. Although this is his first year, he has his program and, for that matter, his future planned. He wants to work with the Boys Clubs of America in some capacity after college. To be best qualified for that work he intends to pursue a double major in physical education and public administration.

With all of the options he surely will have upon graduation, how could he be sure now that he wants a career with the Boys Clubs of America? I asked Ken that question.

"It's important. I've seen how much it can help kids who need help," he said. "Almost half the members—I'm talking about nationally—are from single parent families. Fifty percent are from minority families. Almost 70 percent come from families with an income of less than fifteen thousand dollars a year."

Maggie McBride with daughter Melodi's son, Timothy. Melodi is now the wife of an Episcopal minister; son Cameron is a career Army man now attending the U.S. Army Language Institute in Monterey, Mexico.

Ken McBride with members of the Salem Boys and Girls Club. Ken would like to make a career of staff work in the Boys Clubs of America. "I know it is important," he says.

Ken thought a moment and said, "I know how much the Boys Club helped me."

Ken had brought home a load of clothes to be washed and a load of books for weekend study. It was clear that he was well settled into the routine of being a college student. It was quite a contrast from his whirlwind of activity and attention in the year after he won the National Youth of the Year Award.

"How did you keep your perspective after that?" I asked him. "That must have been heady stuff, the honors, the parades, the speeches, the meetings you attended."

Ken's answer was as levelheaded as I had expected it to be. "I'm proud of what I've accomplished," he said. "But I'd be pretty stupid if I didn't realize how much help I've had. The Boys Club was important. But it was my mother who made the difference. You've talked to her. You know about her. She showed me how to do the things I thought were important. She's something special."

Something special. Maggie McBride and Ken had used the same words about each other, and, of course, they were both right.

WHEN KEN received his great honor in Washington, Maggie McBride was there to see the ceremony in the White House. She was there because a few days before, she had received an envelope containing a round-trip airline ticket to Washington and a check for expenses. The accompanying note was from members of Chemeketa Community College where Maggie works, and it was signed "a few dozen of your fondest admirers."

Renaissance in Detroit

AS WE walked down the hall, students began pouring from classrooms. They talked, laughed, stopped briefly at their lockers, then went on to their next class.

"There aren't any bells," I said.

Our escort from the administrative office laughed. "The teachers know when their classes are over," she said. "The students know when their next class begins. They don't need bells to tell them to be on time."

We were at Renaissance High School on Detroit's West Side, and we were there because we had heard that it is a very special school. The facts and figures we had read before our visit were certainly impressive. The school's curriculum is rigorously college preparatory. Every student takes four years of English, mathematics, science, and social studies, and three years of a foreign language, together with an interesting and challenging array of elective courses. Students carry seven courses each of the eight semesters required for graduation.

The predominantly black, 750-member student body of Renaissance High regularly places first in the city on all standardized tests, and it has been cited by the Council on Great City Schools for its high percentage of National Merit and Achievement scholars. The Renaissance eleventh-grade students do mathematics at a 12.9 grade level, a year and seven months better than the national average. Between 95 and 100 percent of every graduating class goes on to college, and many graduates enter the best universities in the country: Harvard, Yale, Stanford, Massachusetts Institute of Technology, the University of Michigan, to name but a few.

Impressive, indeed, are these accomplishments but no more impressive than what I had seen and heard at the school that morning: an English class seriously and knowledgeably discussing James Joyce's *A Portrait of the Artist as a Young Man,* a science class completely absorbed in experiments in weight and mass. Frank Pavia, the teacher, told me that seventy-two Renaissance High science students had been selected for participation in National Science Foundation projects all over the country during the past summer.

I talked with an eleventh-grade student named Levasseur Tellis; I asked him if he liked Renaissance High and if so, why. "I like it," he said. "I may sound corny, but I like learning, and you can learn here. I like all my subjects, maybe history best right now." I asked him if he had a college in mind, and he said, "Harvard."

Where does Renaissance High get students like Levasseur Tellis? They come from schools all over Detroit, only the very best students as determined by their school records and an achievement test given once a year throughout the city. Just two hundred are selected each year to form the freshman class.

"I was so happy I cried when I was accepted by Renaissance," Nicole Young, another eleventh-grade student told me. I asked her if she was still happy with her choice of schools. "Yes," she said, "I like the special attention. The teachers find time for a one-on-one relationship if we need it." And she added, "I want to go someplace in life."

Nicole lives in a distant part of Detroit. She has to catch a bus at five-thirty in the morning and make several transfers to get to school on time. Many Renaissance High students, I learned, have a one-hour to two-hour commute from their homes to the school.

Frank Pavia with science students. "I love this school," says Pavia. "I may never leave."

A talk with Dr. Beverly Thomas, the principal, helped to put Renaissance High in perspective for me. Dr. Thomas has lived her entire life in Detroit and has been at Renaissance High since it came into existence ten years ago. She talked about some of the problems of Detroit public education, including the fact that out of almost 200,000 students, only slightly more than half are expected to graduate from high school. Renaissance was part of a "schools of choice" plan aimed at fostering a desire for learning.

"From the beginning, Renaissance High represented a dream," she said. "It was a dream and a belief that if you place the right students—those that are academically able and motivated—and the right teachers—those who have the skills and dedication—together in the right environment, then marvelous things can happen.

"We have patterned Renaissance High on the Boston Latin Grammar School. We give the students what we know they need—four years of English, math, science, but we make it enjoyable for them, and we make learning an adventure.

"They are too busy to get into trouble," she said, still talking about the students. "Drugs and drinking take a back seat here. We don't have a drug problem. But they are completely normal teenagers. They love to party and they talk to each other in their own street language. They have at least three languages at their command and know when to shift into classroom English."

Of the Renaissance teachers, Dr. Thomas said, "They are here because they want to be. They apply, and our screening committee selects carefully. We are not clock watchers. We don't come here in the morning with the idea that our workday will be over in eight hours."

Later, I talked to Thelma Dinwiddie, an English teacher who, like Dr. Thomas, has been at Renaissance High since its beginning. "Classroom work where I interact with the kids is what interests me," she said. "It's the thing that *really* interests me. You have to have faith that our regimen, our system, is going to work and then work like the dickens to see that it does. These kids, essentially, are no different from others. We didn't import them from another planet. But they all have one thing: they

Thelma Dinwiddie with English class.

have the ability to focus on education as something important. They have a commitment to learn."

Then Ms. Dinwiddie talked about Renaissance High. "As a school, we haven't been given any special privileges, even though we are expected to excel. Our class size is thirty-five, just as it is in all city schools. We have limited classroom space. In a few minutes you will see me working out in the hall because another teacher has to use this room. We tell students that this experience is a mirror of all life. Success comes from making the most of what you have to work with."

I had already observed that the Renaissance High physical plant was nothing special. The building was old, taken over from Catholic Central High School when that school moved. The laboratories were not full of expensive new equipment. Frank Pavia, the science teacher, had shown me with a touch of pride a large sink he had personally installed in one of the laboratories. Dr. Thomas had put it well when she remarked that Renaissance was an example of what can be done with limited resources and high expectations.

Kenitra Ford, a senior with a 3.92 grade point average, dispelled my concern that with such emphasis on academic achievement, Renaissance High might provide few opportunities for social activities and just plain fun. "It's not that way at all," she said. "I belong to the drama club; I take part in fashion shows; I belong to the girls' pep club."

Just then the school-news broadcast came over the public address system, and the student announcer began by congratulating the girls' volleyball team on a victory the previous night.

"We have a good sports program, too," Kenitra said, "but no football."

Elanjua Current, a ninth grader just getting well started in the school, was very emphatic. "When my friends found out I was coming to Renaissance, they all called it Nerd High," she said, "but it's not. Believe me, it's not."

When I left Renaissance High, I was sure of one thing. It is a school with a difference because every teacher and every student is working to make it that way.

"A Room Called Tomorrow"

IN HIS inaugural address on January 2ᵤ 1989, President George Bush talked about people who make a difference.

"We will make the hard choices," he said, "looking at what we have and perhaps allocating it differently, making our decisions based on honest need and prudent safety. And then we will do the wisest thing of all. We will turn to the only resource we have that in times of need always grows: the goodness and the courage of the American people.

"And I am speaking of a new engagement in the lives of others, a new activism, hands-on, involved—that gets the job done. We must bring in the generations, harnessing the unused talent of the elderly and the unfocused energy of the young. . . .

"I have spoken of a 'thousand points of light'—of all the community organizations that are spread like stars throughout the nation, doing good."

And earlier in his address, the President said, "This is a time when the future seems a door you can walk right through—into a room called tomorrow."

THE PEOPLE I have written about in this book are the kind of people President Bush was talking about. They are special, but they are not unique. Across America hundreds, even thousands, of ordinary citizens are making their lives felt through their work in voluntary organizations, through extra dedication to jobs that help others, through concern for children of poverty, the homeless, the jobless, the handicapped. There can never be enough of these people who make a difference, but they are there, in every state, in every city, probably in every town and village, if we know where to look.

They are the people who will help America open the door to a room called tomorrow.

Bibliography

The stories in this book are based upon direct interviews with the persons written about. In some cases, however, secondary sources were consulted for additional background information. Those sources are listed here.

"I Receive Love"
Doyle, Brian. "I'll Leave When They Bury Me." *U.S. Catholic,* October, 1988.
Lindeman, Les. "The Healing of Soul and Body." *50 Plus,* December, 1987.
Shaw, Bill. "Sister Anne Brooks, Doctor and Nun, Practices without Preaching to the Poor." *People Weekly,* March 23, 1987.
Walsh, Catherine. "Anne Brooks: Doctor and Sister to Mississippi's Poor." *St. Anthony Messenger,* January, 1988.

Helping Hands
Salvatore, Diane. "A Very Special Love Story." *Ladies' Home Journal,* May, 1986.
MacFadyen, J. Tevere. "Educated Monkeys Help the Disabled to Help Themselves." *Smithsonian Magazine,* October, 1986.

A Love Affair with Turtles
McCleery, Patsy R. *The Turtle Lady*. Austin, Texas: Texas Geographic Interests, 1988.
"Saving Our Sea Turtles Is No Easy Task." *The University and the Sea,* Summer, 1982.

The Seventy-Nine-Mile Dream
Stanley, Doug. "Trail Blazer." *The News-Review,* Roseburg, Oregon, August 17, 1986.

Outwitting Señor Coyote
Hart, William. "Camels May Turn Desert Back into Oasis." *New Mexico Magazine,* March, 1989.

The Asian Odyssey of Ron Cowart
Barker, Leslie. "The Heart and Soul of Ron Cowart." *The Dallas Morning News,* September 11, 1988.

The Big House with a Big Heart
De Monnin, Joyce. "This Pope Is a Woman, and She's a Real Saint." *Northwest Women in Business,* March/April, 1986.
Feeny, Patricia. "Hero of the Rough and Tumbled." *Statesman-Journal,* Salem, Oregon, August 9, 1988.
McCarthy, Nancy. "Program of Hope Starved for Funds." *The Oregonian,* Portland, Oregon, February 21, 1988.
Steese, Ellen. "Starting Over." *The Christian Science Monitor,* July 16, 1987.

Hope
Zuniga, Marielena. "The Passionate Friar." *Delaware Today,* December, 1988.

Renaissance in Detroit
Turner, Renée D. "Detroit's Beacon of Achievement." *Ebony,* August, 1988.

In addition to the above articles, the following books were consulted:
Kennedy, Robert. *To Seek a Newer World*. New York: Doubleday & Company, Inc., 1967.
Wecter, Dixon. *The Hero in America*. New York: Charles Scribner's Sons, 1941.

Index

133